Crossing
the Lines

Stories by
Tony Press

ISBN: 978-0-9965405-6-8

Printed in the United States of America

Cover Design: RSCS
Front Cover Photo: Tony Press
Back Cover Photo: Gene Silverman

Big Table Publishing Company
Boston, MA
www.bigtablepublishing.com

The author is forever grateful to the publications in which the following stories first appeared (in some cases, with different titles and/or in different versions).

Boston Literary Magazine: "After the Whistle"
Connotation Press: "Always Present, Always Watching"
Digging Through the Fat: "River Walk in a Railroad Town"
Fiction on the Web: "Café Los Cuiles"
Foundling Review: "The Viper's Smile"
Halfway Down the Stairs: "A Good Day to be Born", "Two Days from the Sea"
JMWW: "Ohio Crossing"
Lichen: "The Viper's Smile"
Linnet's Wings: "At the Station"
Literary Orphans: "Pancakes"
MacGuffin: "Going to Jail Free"
Menda City Review: "A Gentle Rage", "Oregon Trail"
Penmen Review: "Funeral Season"
Qarrtsiluni: "Standing Room Only"
riverbabble: "A Nica in Blighty"
SFWP Quarterly: "Take Me to Your Heart", "Market Day", "Honest as a Sister Can Be", "Not Fifth Avenue", "Hunger"
Shine Journal: "Thank God I Saw Billy Sunday"'
Sleet Magazine: "A Nica in Blighty" ("Playa Malvarrosa" section)
Switchback: "Son of a Father"
Tales from the Courtroom: "Mother, with Child"
Temenos: "Honest as a Sister Can Be"
Toasted Cheese: "Cultural Anthropology", "Always Another Straw", "Mobile on the 214", "Cookie and George"
One Sentence Poems: "Gratitude"

Dedicated to *Karunadevi*

Gratitude

Lost my way again
riding midnight trains of thought
and yet you waited

TABLE OF CONTENTS

"Elvis died on my birthday. My fourteenth. We lived in Delavan then. My mom worked at the club on the lake."

Stirring wretched coffee with a fork while a tinny radio played something that must have been relevant to the assertion, fifty-seven year old Alonzo Johnson wondered how it had been decided, at that moment, in a packed Greyhound diner, that the stranger sharing his two-person table would disclose that particular piece of information. Or, more properly, those pieces, as it wasn't only the Elvis-death-birthday declaration, but there was also Delavan, the mom, and the club. That must have been Hugh Hefner's old place on Lake Geneva. He wondered which was most pertinent.

"Delavan." Alonzo took the safe route, geography. "Is that Walworth County, near Elkhorn?"

"That's right, Walworth," said the younger man. "You can have one foot in Walworth, you know, and the other in Illinois. I guess it sounds better saying 'one foot in Wisconsin, the other in Illinois,' since they're both states. When I was in fourth grade they got our whole class to some park or something once, and they lined us up, left foot Wisconsin, right foot Illinois. My mom's still got the picture somebody took."

Alonzo's eyes focused on the window and the black winter night. He imagined a column of frozen jumping jacks posed forever on the borderline. He had often argued, internally, that state borders, all borders, their entirety, should be marked in a meaningful way: emboldened by massive yellow highlighters, or painted, or chalked, as the white lines on a football field. Sometimes you need to see the lines.

"My mom liked Elvis a lot, had all his music, but it was this friend of hers who was the fanatic. She was staying with us that summer, on her way to 'California, or maybe Colorado.' She was crazy in love with him. I was sitting right next to her when she heard it on the television. She looked like a clock someone threw out a window."

The abrupt resumption of words shoved away Alonzo's image, and he mourned the loss. He would like to see that photograph as it sat on an aged mother's piano, or, more likely, in a dusty box in a closet, though he suspected it wouldn't match the one in his mind. Smashed clocks, however, were something he had really seen.

"She was devastated. She dressed in black for a week, but I guess all she had that was black were these tight leotard dance things, and real short shorts…hot pants maybe? It was weird. She looked like something out of Hollywood. I couldn't stop staring at her, and she was as old as my mom. I was even thinking about her in bed."

Both sides of the tiny table paused at the revelation, giving it its due.

"She never left the house, just played those records over and over and over. One night, when my mom was pulling a double-shift, she told me to sing–no, she didn't tell me, she ordered me–to sing 'Love Me Tender' to her. I don't even know if she knew I could sing or not. I hadn't sung a word since they kicked me out of choir the year before, for smoking."

Smoking at what, thirteen? Alonzo himself had started at fifteen. After a few desultory attempts over forty years, he had quit completely, hadn't smoked in eight months.

"It was the one she played the most, I heard it literally thirty-five times, maybe more, that week."

It was rare to hear the word "literally" used correctly. Alonzo believed he had just experienced it.

"'Sing it to me at midnight, on the back porch.' That's exactly what she said. She went to the porch–it was screened in, that's where she was sleeping–and came back with a scrap of paper with the lyrics. They were in handwriting. Hers, I guess. She put it in my hand and didn't say another word, just walked back out through the porch to the yard. I took it to my room, but I could watch her out my window, about twenty yards behind the house, sitting cross-legged on the hood of her old Pontiac, smoking and staring out somewhere. For the entire time, almost two hours, she just sat there, her eyes fixed. I angled my neck, but I couldn't see what she was looking at."

Stars, Alonzo explained to himself. She was searching southern Wisconsin's endless summer sky, certain that solace could be found if only she knew where to look.

"Of course, I knew it already, the song, I'd heard it so much that week. I especially like the line in the middle: *Take me to your heart.'* But I did practice it a bunch of times. At first just to myself, then a little louder, and once, after I shut my window, at full strength until I knew I had it the way I wanted. Then I waited, but double-wide awake, keeping an eye on the clock, and keeping an eye on her, too, sitting right where she'd been the first time I looked."

Alonzo stretched his right arm across his chest to knead his left shoulder. He lifted his coffee but replaced it without touching the cup to his lips.

"At two minutes of, I was still watching her. She slid off the hood and started in to the porch. I stuffed the lyrics into my jeans pocket even though I knew I didn't need them, and I went to her. I remember I was barefoot, and I had on a Packer jersey, but for some reason I can't remember which one. I had three or four different ones. I wish I knew."

Alonzo had a fleeting memory of a refrain: "I went to her." How much, in four words?

"When I got there, she was standing at the far end, by the head of the day bed we had, the one that she used. She motioned me to stay at the other end, so I was standing just inside the screen door. Next to her was a circle of candles on a little wrought-iron table. She lit every candle. Then she spoke, but when she did, I could barely hear her. She said 'Now. Now, please.' She closed her eyes and I sang. Maybe they were already closed the whole time, I don't know."

Even on a windless August night, the flames would have danced, sending gentle shadows to the fake-wood paneling of the summer porch.

"I nailed that song. I had a band later, and I still sing sometimes, but I've never hit it like that. About thirty seconds after I stopped, she opened her eyes and kind of tiptoed to where I was standing. She put both her hands on my face and kissed me for as long as the song had lasted.

I had kissed before, but I hadn't, after all. In those minutes with her, with her tears pouring all down my face, I realized why and how grownups kissed.

She pulled back, traced the line of my jaw with one finger, and then rested it for a split-second on my peach-fuzz mustache. Sometimes I can still feel that finger. Then she picked up her little suitcase, walked past me into the yard, and drove away."

He shrugged, took a few breaths, continued. "I've had three marriages, two of them good ones. My wife and I still surprise each other. I have no complaints. None. But that kiss will stay with me forever. Up to then, I'd just been waiting, you know, like you wait for a bus that might never show up."

Alonzo Johnson took a large last swallow of cold coffee, grateful as it graced his tongue and teeth, swept both checks from the table, paid the cashier, added a generous tip, and, next to the cash register, found a cigarette machine. He pumped quarters into the slot until a crisp pack of Camels dropped to the tray. Grabbing a nameless book of matches from a bowl on the counter, he strode outside into the chill, his breath immediately visible, the pack already open and a Camel between his lips. Instinctively locating the darkest corner of the parking lot, he leaned against the base of a utility pole, its iciness cutting his thin jacket to the small of his back. Amid the constellations he was easily able to locate, as he struck his first match in 240 days, the screened-in porch in Delavan, the little blue suitcase and the stringed handbag, and the red tail lights, one brighter than the other, heading west across the bright yellow lines.

Going to Jail Free

They laughed when they saw it. *Welcome to Denton, Home of Beautiful Women* crowed the largest billboard they'd seen in five hundred miles, but as the van dropped from highway to neighborhood speeds, neither saw anything to justify the claim. In fact, Robby didn't spot a single female, much less a beautiful one, on the late afternoon sidewalks. He also didn't see the little red car until metal hit metal. He did see as its left headlight clattered across the blacktop, its silver rim catching the last shimmers of the sun. It caromed up and over the opposite curb, spinning three times, then rested upon the town square's thirsty grass.

Descending from opposite sides of the van, they did not need nametags to announce: "Hi, we're hippies from California." No doubt they looked like refugees from Woodstock who had descended into Texas, and he was thinking it may have been a big mistake. Combined, they weighed less than the mountainous man still inside the victimized car. As he looked more closely, the guy's height, too, seemed to double theirs. Jake, the driver and registered owner of the bus, wasn't sure what had happened, but had his hands on his head, the international sign for "my fault." Robby had actually seen something as they began the wide right turn, but he hadn't spoken in time. He was busy imagining the beautiful women and also figuring out when they would reach the Mississippi River, which would mark the furthest east he had been since he was five. Thus, the right turn, while not grossly negligent, had been negligent enough, because the cherry-red 1957 MG Midget had already staked out the curb lane as its own.

The deputy walked with a confidence that didn't require a swagger. He wore khaki pants and a matching shirt, a Sam Browne belt with pistol and nightstick, and he was hatless in the September heat.

"Barlow, what happened to you now?" Intimately. Softly. Had he heard right? Had they, owing solely to his muddled navigation, surfaced in a town in Texas where everyone, even the police, really did know everyone?

He also never would have guessed it possible that a 6'2", 265-

pound man could fit in a '57 Midget, but this man Barlow could. It turned out he had played high school football with three of the town's deputy sheriffs, including the one ambling from the courthouse lawn.

"Evening boys. Perhaps you two could kindly show me some identification. And vehicle registration." He continued to speak gently, bypassing question marks, leaving no question that his words were mandates. "I don't think we need to worry about moving these vehicles just yet." He nodded to the big man and said "maybe you could fetch that headlight of yours so some little barefooted kid doesn't cut himself." Barlow extricated himself and retrieved the missing part.

"Jacob Jamison, Seal Beach, California. Robert Jefferson, Fresno, California. My goodness, if my brother was on duty tonight, he'd be shouting into the two-way: 'We got some genuine outside agitators here in front of the courthouse!' He feels cheated that nobody's ever tried to foment revolution on his watch."

Somehow they exchanged glances, despite keeping their eyes glued to the ground.

"But don't worry boys. I'm not my brother. Why don't you sit on our Memorial Bench over here while Barlow tells me what transpired." Through sporadic 265-pound sobs, the lament poured forth like that mighty Mississippi. He told Hank–his buddy, the cop–how, as he damn well knew, he had scraped and suffered to get this car street-safe, and how he had chased down and personally installed nothing-but-original parts inside and out, and how, how difficult it had been to get the headlights, the finishing touch, the "piece-de-resistance." Despite himself, Robby automatically noted "Pizza Day Resistance" as a good name for a band. And when had those headlights gone on, so carefully, so lovingly, so exquisitely? Today! He hadn't even taken a picture.

It was a sweet car. If Gerber made cars, this would be a Gerber's. Ten years older than the bus, it looked ten times newer, cleaner, better.

There was one flaw. An eye was knocked out. That was the left headlight, the "bug-eye." In a highway of the blind, was the one-eyed car still king? That side of the little tyke's face was undeniably ugly

14

right now, wouldn't pass any baby food audition.

"How about your proof of insurance, Mr. Jamison. Everything else looks in order. Of course, I'll have to write you up for an inattentive turn, but that won't run you too much."

"Here it is, sir." Jake's voice quivered like a car radio with a loose knob, and he inhaled deeply as the deputy examined the insurance stub.

"Well, actually, it appears we do have a problem. Mr. Jamison, today is September 9th but your coverage expired on August 28th. That is decidedly a problem."

"I can explain that, sir. It really hasn't expired. It's just that I haven't received my new card yet. I paid it way back when it was due, before it was due, but we've been on the road and nobody at my new house has sent it to me. I'm sure it's sitting in a pile of mail in L.A. I've got a bunch of roommates, but you don't know how flaky they can be."

"That may be, and it may not be, but right now, you and I are going to walk to the other side of that lawn and into my office. You may move your van to the side of the road first. I trust you won't do anything silly when you're behind the wheel."

Robby stood by. The van was parked was directed and they walked with the deputy to the office. The word "office" sounded suspiciously like a euphemism for jail, and as they entered the double-doors he was not overjoyed to be proved right. There was a sitting area with a few plastic chairs, a soda machine, a counter with two desks behind it, and to the left, visible as day (pizza or otherwise), were four jail cells, just like in the movies. In each cell was a cot with a mattress and a blanket, but one cell had bunk-cots, if that's what jail bunk beds were called. A bald man in an orange jail jumpsuit occupied one cell but didn't look up from his book.

"I just can't let you go without proof that poor Barlow's going to get compensated. If we had that insurance company in town, I'd call up the agent, but we don't. It's not that I haven't heard of your company, but they just aren't anywhere around here. But you can use that pay phone in the corner. If you can reach your agent, maybe we'll be okay."

He looked at the clock. What time was it in California? It was hard to read time on the road. Even in California it was pretty late for office hours.

They pooled dimes and nickels and Jake dialed the number on the back of his expired card. David Parr, certified agent, was the get-out-of-jail-free card. If Mr. Parr happened to be in the office.

He wasn't.

Jake reminded him: "It's just a little place in that strip mall, you know, where Daydream Records is." He had an image of offices and shops in the sleepy corridor that housed the excellent used-record store. He didn't remember ever seeing any of those offices open.

"I'm just getting a recording—wait, there's something else. Give me a pen!" Jake cradled the receiver and scribbled furiously. "No! It cut off. Give me more money." He re-dialed, this time poised for the information. "It's saying another number that can be used for emergencies."

It was agreed that it was an emergency and they employed the last of the change. "It's another machine!" Jake's body slumped, his face bereft of color. "Yes, yes, I want to leave a message! This is Jacob Jamison, my policy number is 156-1623-515, and I need you to call me, no, to call—where should they call?" Robby looked at the sheriff who swiftly handed him a business card. "Give them that second number there, that'll come right here."

With the second card in an increasingly damp left hand, Jake read the Texas phone number, enunciating each digit, then repeated it, closing the call with: "please, it's an emergency," and then slumped to a plastic chair and stared into nothing.

Robby asked the sheriff. "What now?"

"We wait. If we get a call back this evening, and they say the magic words, then you're both on your way. If not, then only you are on your way. Your friend will be a guest of the county."

He couldn't remember where they'd planned to be tonight. They tried not to drive too much after dark because the van's weak battery struggled to power the headlights. There was a big county map under glass on the counter and someone had told them about a park with a creek, but the name had escaped through the back door of his brain. Euless? Grapevine? Back to the clock, each tick a step closer to his buddy behind bars, his buddy who sat, head in hands, elbows on knees, eyes open but shut.

An hour passed. Ninety minutes. The phone rang, jolting the two off their seats, but it was Mrs. Hank, asking for cigarettes and a box of diapers. Mr. Hank himself, after writing up his report, was reading the paper and listening to the radio that connected him with another sheriff.

He asked if he could borrow part of the paper. "It ain't but two sections," the sheriff lamented, "but here's sports. You ever play football?"

"No," he admitted, thinking for the first time in his life what a good thing it would be to have football on his resume, "but I watch it all the time. Last week we were sleeping in a parking lot on campus in Norman, Oklahoma and the U.S.C. band marched right by blasting their fight song, heading for the stadium. That was a bad way to wake up. I always did hate U.S.C."

"Well, I was for 'em on Saturday, 'cuz I hate O.U. Texans are born to hate O.U."

"Me and Jake went–go–to U.C.L.A. We're just off for a while. For us, U.S.C. means 'University of Second Choice,' or sometimes 'University of Spoiled Children.'"

"That's good. We don't really have that for Oklahoma. They're just assholes, I guess. I played high school and we were pretty good, too. Barlow would have been all-state but he tore up his knee senior year. We still won section." He paused, honoring the memory. "You see that billboard outside of town, the one that says 'Home of Beautiful Women?'"

He nodded.

"That sign's really for the college here, 'cuz they had girls win Miss

Texas two years in a row, and once, some girl made it to the Miss Universe deal. It's just a branch of the big one down in Austin, of course. When we had two-a-day practices before the season started senior year, there was one day we were just dragging our sorry behinds–man it was hot–and coach, Coach Logan stopped everything and put us on the bus. I didn't know where we were going but I figured he was going to yell at us for dogging it, and maybe take us out of town and make us run back. But he drove us over to the college. We considered him an old man, but he wasn't even fifty. We got there, right outside this grassy area in front of one of the girls' dormitories, and they were all out there, reading and sun-bathing, and he tells us: 'You see that? You see that! Look at that! Smell it! College pussy! That's what a goddamn football scholarship is all about. That's why you can't be weak! Just look at those girls.'"

"Did you get one?"

"A scholarship? No, but when I worked security out there before this job, I did get some private tutoring, if you catch my drift. Before I got married." And again he paused, his eyes far from work. "That's where I met my wife, too, and she could be on that billboard."

Silence reclaimed the room, but this time without the harshness.

Ten minutes later, the bald man in cell number one called out to Hank, and the two joined into a lengthy conversation. He tried to eavesdrop but had no idea what the inmate was saying. He didn't think it was English but every so often it sounded exactly like English. Was he talking about the Lusitania? Louisiana? Lucid dreams? The conversation ended as fast as it had begun.

The sheriff turned to him again: "If you're here on Saturday, there's a circus in town. They come every year, it's pretty good."

"I knew it!" His face brightened for the first time in hours. "This morning I swore I saw a giraffe on the back of a flatbed truck, but that guy over there was sleeping and didn't believe me. Damn, it got so I wasn't even sure myself."

"I don't know, that could have been part of it."

"Oh, yeah, it had to be. A guy was riding on the back with it, and

18

every time they came to an overpass, he'd tug on the rope and the giraffe would duck its head. Man, I'm never going to forget that again. I'll tell my grandchildren about that."

The sheriff said he was going home at eleven, so if anything were to happen, it had to happen before then. Jake was sprawled and half-asleep. Robby paced, willing his mind away from the wall clock. Willing, but not able. The clock, itself near-exhausted by the weight of its burden, continued to tick.

The phone rang at 10:33. Sheriff Hank listened, spoke, listened, spoke, took some notes, and when he said, "sounds good," Robby wanted to hug him.

"I'm satisfied," he smiled. "And if I'm satisfied, the state of Texas is satisfied. The ticket's only twenty-three dollars. Pay it before you leave and don't worry about a court date."

"Sheriff, I need to ask you something. I'm exhausted, my friend's a wreck, and there's really no place we can get to now. Can we stay here? I mean, in a cell, so we can get some sleep?"

"They didn't tell me about that one at cop school." He produced a large ring of keys. "But I don't see any reason why not. That'll even cancel your friend's ticket, call it 'time-served.' But one thing you need to understand."

"What's that?"

"No breakfast."

In the morning, as promised, they did not get breakfast. But they had slept, and conversed with the real inmate, a trucker with significant warrant problems who said he was from Accomplice, Georgia. They looked blank until he said: "Don't you boys know who discovered America?"

Although not fed, they did, thanks to Hank, who surprisingly turned up at eight, get "one free pick" from prisoners' lost and found, and he quickly snagged a black cowboy hat. His partner rummaged hungrily but unsuccessfully for real Texas cowboy boots and had to settle for a faded "Hook 'em Horns" baseball cap. "This just ain't my town."

"If you can pay a little, stop at Darla's on the east side of town. They got great boots, the real thing. They have that 'beautiful women' sign over there, too, just before you get to it from the other side, and a buddy of mine from Dallas is convinced it means Darla and her sisters."

Following directions highlighted by Hank on a brand-new map, he pulled into Darla's broad parking lot. Jake leaped from the van, his eyes wide at the display of shiny boots in the window. "There they are! Just what I've been wanting since forever." They fit perfectly. And then Barlow strolled out from the back room.

The boots thudded onto the hardwood floor. Jake relocated his voice. "Man, I'm so sorry about yesterday. But you're okay about the insurance, right? You know you'll be covered completely. The sheriff...he told you?"

"Yeah, it's cool," said the giant. "I was pissed, but I'm a big boy. It's like that saying."

"Tomorrow is another day?"

"*Gone with the Wind*, right? That works, but I was thinking of 'what doesn't destroy you makes you stronger.'"

Barlow rang up the sale and introduced them to two of his much smaller, and much prettier, sisters. The boots were perfect for his pal: sharp lines and three shades of brown, and now he was two inches taller, walking on unseen clouds, lighter by twenty-five dollars.

Barlow walked out with them to take a fresh look at the van. First, the outside scarred with dings and dents, and then he peered inside, the back strewn with camping gear and baseball bats and the scattered debris of their time on the road. He took the larger of the two bats, the Henry Aaron Louisville Slugger, and ran his hands along the grain. It had never looked smaller. Robby was looking back at the store and the sisters when his road companion had this bright idea:

"Barlow, back in Boulder, my pal here got rejected three nights in a row by what your sheriff friend might call 'educated' chicks. Just before we pulled out, I handed him that very bat, and that's where, in the middle of the sliding door, that deep dent came from. In honor of your little car, do you want to take a swing at the other side?"

Three nights later, parked on a western bluff, the tantalizing current of the Mississippi just below, they marveled at the full moon shining through "Barlow's Gap," another good name for a band. The guy had one hell of a swing.

Market Day

At least one Wednesday a month they drove the thirty-miles south into the valley and Ocotlán de Morelos. It wasn't that Oaxaca itself didn't have sprawling open-air, and closed-air, markets; indubitably, there were several, and possibly one for every day of the week. But Sally and Anna and most of their neighbors, whether ex-pat or local, preferred this one. The market in Ocotlán was the one they'd bring out-of-town visitors to, and each time they did they reminded themselves to make it a habit, and not save it for special occasions. Sometimes they stopped on the way down in the *pueblito* of San Martín Tilcajete, to browse and sometimes purchase more of the carefully painted wood carvings–the *alebrijes*–the delicate *animalitos* that danced on Anna's bookshelves at home. "Every trip your office looks more zoo than workplace," Sally told her.

But once in Ocotlán and the market, strolling *dos de la mano* through live goats and pigs and chickens waiting to be selected for a festive meal, plants and baskets and fruits and vegetables and kitchen implements and sandals and socks and all other manner of clothing, and all of that was before they got to the pottery and tools and– increasingly, electronics, it was a splendid mix of beauty and practicality. More than once they'd had their pictures taken with the woman who sold *chocolate* and was a dead-ringer, and dressed as such, for Frida Kahlo. It was a long way from Chadron, Nebraska.

Sometimes there were entertainers just outside the market, between the square and the art museum, and today Anna squeezed Sally's hand as soon as she saw the banner: *Los Hermanos Rosales.*

It was a tiny traveling circus, not quite as small as a flea circus but small enough that all the performers and all of the gear fit inside and in the back of a small pick-up, but it was a circus nonetheless, with a tent pitched on the corner near the HSBC bank. The tent was barely bigger than an REI family-style, and it was open on three sides.

They watched, first in amusement, then in awe, as one of the five or six or eight *Los Hermanos Rosales*, the one with a braided ponytail, casually juggled an axe, an egg, a frog and an iguana.

Anna whispered to Sally, "What, no partridge? No pear tree?" Sally—cameras in each of her carrier pants pockets—started shooting. These would be good.

After the juggling came two tumblers with more energy than grace and *Los Hermanos* knew it because their clown re-entered, screamed silently at the tumblers, knocked them to the ground, and proceeded to kick each one off the large rug that was their stage. The rug was probably Walmart, a shame given the classic Teotitlán del Valle rugs widely available in the market and in shops and showrooms for miles around. Just last week they had spent twelve hundred U.S. on a 10x15 that was alive with reds and blues, birds and triangles, all dancing within a classic Zapotec pattern—they had watched it come off the loom. But as Sally often reminded Anna, if everybody and her sister back in the states got to eat, sleep, and breathe Walmart, why shouldn't similarly misguided citizens of the State of Oaxaca have the same opportunity.

"Y ahora, *and now*, la estrella de las estrellas, *the star of stars,* our very own sister, *nuestra propia hermana."*

Sally gasped as the slender young woman emerged from the tent. She could have been twenty-five, could have been fifteen, but even in the shimmering B-movie-version gypsy-outfit, she was the image of Jenna: Jenna, the one saving grace of East Jesus, Colorado, almost two decades ago. They were both eighteen, Sally and Jenna. Sally was stuck there for a month with her all-male crew—they grudgingly admired her strength but they would never be buddies—while they yanked out and replaced three busted pipelines at the edge of town. Jenna was stuck for a lifetime. A lifetime that would not see nineteen.

Sally swallowed, grabbed Anna's hand, and watched as the woman who looked like Jenna walked into the center. The announcing brother shouted even louder but Sally missed what he said. The small crowd surrounded the rug.

A brother tapped on an ancient drum. Another riffed on some kind of flute, like the ones in the Peruvian bands that often played in the Zocalo. A third, the worst of the tumblers, gravely placed at the feet of the woman who was not Jenna a long, thin wooden box. He stood up, bowed once, and backed his way off of the rug. The gypsy-dress rippled in the breeze as the woman bent with impossible grace. Her knowing fingers found the spring that released the lid. Sally tugged Anna closer.

In the box, sheathed in velvet with only the handles and hasps visible, were three knives. First, a knife with a four-inch blade; second, a similar but longer one, with a blade about eight inches long; and third, what could only be called a sword. It had to be a foot and a half long. Sally realized her own breathing had stopped and she willed its return. Anna placed one hand on the small of Sally's back. With her other hand she caressed Sally's right hand.

The four-inch knife, studded with rubies, was first to be employed. The crowd continued to grow, its shuffling feet raising dust that floated above their heads and settled on hats, faces, shoulders. The sister stood tall, arched her back, and opened her mouth impossibly wide. She held the knife inches above her lips. Soon the knife disappeared, rested for a moment somewhere between and beyond those lips, before it returned into the daylight, the gems again brilliant. As slowly as she had removed it, she placed it back into its sheath and returned it to the box. One spectator shouted but stopped in mid-note. Another sobbed. Jenna-not-Jenna closed her eyes and stood in silent yoga sun-salutation. The crowd waited, an alchemy of patience and desperate anticipation. Sally counted heartbeats. Three minutes faded from present to past. Then the next knife, this one's handle smothered with emeralds. The action duplicated the first, but the blade, twice as long, reduced the first effort to child's play. An *abuelita* swooned into the arms of a stranger who kept her from falling but never took his eyes from *la estrella de las estrellas*. Again, fearful beauty ascended from the angelic neck, the throat of magic.

Despite, or perhaps because of the stillness, the hush, more people came, doubling, then doubling again, the size of the crowd. Moving as minutely as possible, men wiped sweat and grime with red bandanas. This time the wait was five minutes.

Sally's eyes moved like fingers along the woman's face. She traced the lines of the chin, flickered along the lips, ran them down each arm from shoulder to elbow to fingertips, and paused. She dared touch the astonishing neck before slipping effortlessly to the chest, hidden by the silk blouse. Her eyes feathered the breasts, just a whisper of contact. "Feels like God's grace," Jenna had said. Anna now stood fully behind her, against her, arms wrapped around Sally's waist. She took both of Sally's hands in her own, fingers interlocked.

Sally took a deep breath. She allowed the fingers of her eyes to trace the scar across the heart, the scar that would have formed had Jenna survived, but Jenna hadn't wanted that. Just as she hadn't wanted Sally to disappear, her begging insufficient to keep Sally in East Jessup, and she knew she herself would not leave, could not leave, as long as her mother lived. Not until her mother's death. Or her own. The knife she used was a mere three inches, rusty rather than jeweled, but it worked.

The sword was now in her hand. The sword and her right arm formed a glimmering L in the cloudless sky.

Sally screamed, "No!" No one moved, nor spoke. The sword, too, remained in place.

Anna cradled Sally into a sitting position, squeezed her hands and gave her a quick kiss.

"Hold on," Anna said.

Next she approached the oldest *hermano*, an uncle or father if they were related at all. She engaged him in private, rapid conversation. The man raised a huge hand in the air and requested continued silence. All obeyed: the sword-woman, the brothers, and the people, who appeared now more as penitents than circus-goers.

Anna and the man entered the bank. Time suspended its circuit. Butterflies stilled. Lifetimes later, Anna and the man re-appeared, each shielding eyes against the sun. Wordlessly he removed the sword from the compliant young woman–she did not break pose–inserted it into its velvet glove, and handed it to Anna.

Anna drove in silence, the sword nestled on the back seat with the papaya, mango, and jicama, all purchased before they knew the circus had come to town. Sally's eyes were open but she could have been sleeping. At home she did sleep for most of the afternoon.

Out on the redwood deck, beneath the stars that filled the summer sky, they shared a blanket on the bench as the temperature cooled. The sword lay inside like a sleeping dog. It was still wrapped in newspapers–*Noticias* and *El Imparcial.* Anna had already contacted the artisan who would build a case for it, for their bedroom wall.

The night yawned before their eyes.

"She had never seen a sword swallower. Shit, she had never seen Denver." Sally stopped, sipped from Anna's mojito–she had declined one of her own–and started again.

"Jenna never once got out of East Jessup–East Jesus according to the locals, all 143 of them–and she wouldn't know a nail salon from a cell block, but God, her fingers. They were flawless, gorgeous, longer than mine. People thought she was a frail little thing, but she wasn't. She was so tough, but…I really never will forget her."

Anna kissed her. "I'll just make that #412 on the list of reasons why I love you."

Cultural Anthropology

The morning of the last class of that summer session–the university campus aching to empty for the remaining weeks of August, 1970–Professor Cortez presented "an old friend," introducing him as Charles Culbertson. He told us that his friend, a colleague for many years, would deliver a unique perspective on courtship, marriage, and sexuality among certain traditional Native American cultures. Like Cortez, Culbertson was probably 40, and equally tanned. In all other respects, he was the antithesis of him. He wore drab, baggy suit pants, a mismatched tired sport-coat, and a wrinkled shirt that had a faint memory of white. He was no more than five foot six and Cortez was a good six-four. His backpack, open on the floor beside him, contained a liquor store paper bag out of which he sipped, furtively at first, but more openly as his talk progressed. He spoke with an inflection that strayed from Latin American to Eastern European. Neither sounded true. Although he dangled intriguing phrases like "temporary adoration," "sense penetration," and "descending into the power," his talk lacked compass and meandered from one obscure reference to another. Thirty minutes in, as if a timer had sounded, he stopped, giggled, swooped up his belongings, and scurried off the stage, out the side door into the sunlit parking lot. The door slammed behind him.

Cortez walked to the vacated podium and invited response. Little was offered and the discussion faded quickly. Cortez burst into an extravagant smile: "Actually, Charles Culbertson isn't his real name. That was Carlos Castaneda. It's been a good summer. Thank you. If you turned in a postcard, you'll get your grades in about a week." And he was gone.

What the fuck? We didn't know if it was true. We didn't even know where to begin thinking about it. Worse, April, sitting next to me, had never heard of Castaneda. Since then, I've never investigated, never felt any urgency to seek the truth of it, but the incident has never quite faded. Then and now, it seemed an appropriate coda to the course, and to what was to be our last night of the summer. Fall classes were racing in with a vengeance but this year I wasn't playing. I had a ride-board connection to Madison, Wisconsin, where a friend of a friend would house me for a few days. After that…who knew? It was all waiting for me. For three months. After the three months, it would be back to school to save my student deferment. In another year, I'd have a degree. Maybe the war would be over.

I had met April in the front row of that Cultural Anthropology course, the day Cortez lectured on something about "titan realms of the mind." I always sat in front rows figuring if I was going to be there, I might as well *be* there. If I wanted to sleep, I stayed home. Cortez worked the room, hair hanging to his shoulders, tight black shirt painted on his torso, blue jeans clinging to his long legs. His boots, which April and I called "Spanish rock & roll boots," punctuated the smooth floor with each observation and challenge. Daily for six weeks, 120 students packed the room. It was the class you'd invite a visiting friend to see. He was also rumored to be rich—once we saw him drive a bright red British sports car. He was so fantastic it crossed my mind April might have been looking for him when she searched my face. I couldn't have blamed her.

Cortez was a scholar of the world. I played the role of a student. I did want to travel some day but Vietnam was not high on my list.

Bob Dylan was a titan, as were Jim Morrison and Mick Jagger. Was I? April's eyes, trained on me the next morning, made me feel that she thought it possible, and it was a good feeling. She sat cross-legged at the foot of my bed, her girlish body covered by one of my earliest Grateful Dead t-shirts. Though the shirt had been designed for someone much bigger, the shirt rode up when she shifted slightly, allowing a glimpse of her still damp pubic hair, and I stirred once more beneath the crumpled sheets.

She was eighteen and I was almost twenty-one. I had logged three-plus years of college and she had just begun in June, one week after graduating from high school. It was a significant gap.

She was the first girl I'd slept with more than twice. And for the last three weeks of summer school, she had been staying with me four

28

nights a week, going home to her parents for the weekend, and then to her dorm for Sunday night. Her parents assumed, we assumed, that she was always at the dorm when she wasn't with them.

On my bed that last morning she kept looking, as if she might forget everything the instant I crossed into Idaho. Even though I was the one leaving, she was the first out from under the covers. My ride was due. I remembered an earlier summer, still in high school, when I'd taught myself to sleep naked. It was strange, to not wear pajama pants or underwear, but I knew that someday, soon, I hoped, I'd want to be comfortably naked with a girl.

"This is like *Romeo and Juliet*," April said, playfully or seriously, I couldn't tell. I often couldn't. The movie had been our first date.

"Remember," she said, "he knows it's time to leave, and he gets up, but she can't stand it, and convinces him to stay a little longer. Let's see, what did she do?" To my delight, she remembered.

Jesus, that guy was mad, but then he was laughing, when we staggered out to his car, my shirt in my hand, after ten minutes of honking. He dropped April at her dorm and we were on our way.

In five days I was in Madison, smoking dope in a brown-shingled house that supposedly once was Fighting Bob La Follette's. After a few blissful days, I recognized the seduction of trading one campus town for another, so I put some effort into the next step. I found a job, and a room, in Janesville, forty miles south (and much farther still, it felt, especially without a car, from the hypnotic pull of student life). I worked, to my thrill, in a real blue-collar job, on an assembly line at Parker Pen. In postcards home I made cryptic references to "developing alliances with the proletariat."

My room was over a garage on a quiet street midway between downtown and the plant, in walking distance of a sweet little park. I crossed it to get to my bus stop, the playground packed with little kids, mothers and some fathers, and grandparents. It was a place a grandmother would love, and I readily accepted its comforts.

I was making more money than I knew possible, drinking Point beer, and even playing softball. Parker Pen had four teams in the city league and I got on one that played on the increasingly autumnal Wednesday evenings. Kirby's Bar on Main Street, its walls lined with Green Bay Packer pennants and photos, was our team's post-game site. If you went out the back way, beyond the pay phone and the toilets, you could stand, carefully, above the darkness of the Rock River. If you were drunk, you were a fool to get close.

It was from Kirby's that I usually called April, the time difference working in our favor. I'd grab a bottle and set up camp at the phone with an ashtray filled with change. We talked for as many quarters and dimes as I had, with a little sighing and heavy breathing thrown in. In my time in Janesville I was just so happy with the whole situation that other than those calls I had no need for female company.

One Wednesday night, after seven innings of body-numbing softball in rapidly declining temperatures —"how can any third baseman in the world throw a ball with hands this cold?"—we were a particularly loud and raucous group, making the place even more our own than ever.

The "hello" sounded wrong. I thought for a second it was her roommate, even though that unknown entity had not once answered since I'd begun calling from Wisconsin.

"April? Are you okay?"

"Yeah, yeah, it's just that…" I heard nothing more.

"What is it, babe? You don't sound good. What's up?"

"I'm pregnant."

I can't speak for a pin or a feather, but you do hear it when a bottle drops. It didn't break because it had been low in my hand when it fell, but it thundered on the concrete floor, and it was the only sound either of us heard for a long, expensive time. Only the phone company was happy.

"Shit, babe, are you sure? Forget that, that was stupid. You are. What, what…how are you?"

"Not so good." I'd never heard her cry. "It's so scary."

"What…who…does anyone else know? What are you doing? What are we going to do? What do you want?"

"It's all set up. It'll be taken care of next week. Honey," the crying increased to sobs. "Honey, can you come back?"

"I'll be there as fast as I can. It might take a couple of days, but I'll be there, I promise."

"I love you."

"I love you. Don't worry."

"Hurry."

"I'll be there as soon as I can. We'll take care of it. I'm with you all the way. I love you. I'll see you soon."

It took two tries to get the receiver back where it belonged. I picked up the empty bottle and walked out the back door to the river steps. The wind laughed as it whipped through my thin *Parker Pen* jersey, and I screamed the word "fuck" louder than I'd ever screamed anything before. I made my best throw of the night, heaving the bottle as far south as I could, maybe all the way to Beloit.

I could have made my excuses, hustled back to my rented room, and begun the process of getting myself back to Seattle, but I didn't. Not right away.

I stopped first at the bar for another beer, and more, for commiseration. How could this happen to me? I'd been riding so high. Why hadn't she taken care of things? Why hadn't I? I was older, maybe I should have been more responsible, but we both were so careful. It wasn't supposed to happen like this.

My teammates were several beers ahead. My face invited questions. Questions led to answers. Answers led to more beer. More beer led to sarcasm, irony, ribaldry, raunchiness, drunken wit. Soon there were toasts to my virility, cheers for the size and skill of my tool, hip-hip-hoorays for April's fertile delta. Ballplayers competitively imagined, and loudly described, "April-the-Acrobat." We argued the best ways to tell, just by looking, how juicy a girl was. Then we got to their smells, their flavors, and the curse of pubic hair between the teeth.

Things did not improve–Kirby simply locked the door to prevent newcomers–as we reduced all women to manipulating cunts, as we hilariously topped each other's suspicions of April's motives, as Ricky said "that's another reason to stick with sheep," and Carl added "damn it, if they can bleed, they can breed." But when Darrell, our catcher, team captain, and my forty-five-year-old line supervisor and I chanted "4-F, 4-F– Find 'em, Feel 'em, Fuck 'em, Forget 'em," part of me realized that I was behaving worse than I knew possible, and that if in that bar, or watching or listening through some unknown window, were any girl or woman who actually knew me, or was related to me, or might ever meet me, I would have thrown myself in the Rock River and prayed never to surface. It was the worst night I'd ever witnessed, and I was right in the middle of it.

In the midst of it, they did take a collection and I was able to leave for Seattle the next afternoon. In the morning I quit my room, quit my job, signed over my last check to pay the guys back, and threw up. Repeatedly. I was nauseous on the bus to Chicago, and then the flight, through delays and bad weather, duplicated the morning's agony. I spent most of the red-eye hanging over the cramped toilet.

We spent Friday together. She had indeed set everything up and the abortion was going to be first thing Tuesday. She'd been resourceful, gotten herself on benefits so it would be almost free, and most importantly, her parents wouldn't know. We didn't talk a whole lot, just walked around campus holding hands. Her body didn't look any different but her face was a mess. She said she felt like shit. I was pretty weak myself, but I was smart enough to shut up about that, and she didn't have much energy for me anyway. She was, as she had in the summer, heading home for the weekend. We would see each other on Monday, and then drive together to the clinic on Tuesday. She had arranged to borrow a friend's car that I could drive.

Although there were plenty of floors and couches I could sleep on, I didn't much want to be in Seattle and I especially didn't want to tell anyone why I was back. Maybe I feared a repeat of Kirby's. It happened that my mother's birthday was that Sunday so I decided to hop a bus down to Portland to surprise her. For all she knew, her baby boy was still in Wisconsin. The idea of another bus ride made me cringe, but the thought of making someone happy, especially my mother, really appealed to me. I could get back on Monday, and nobody, especially mom, needed to know the real reason I was in town.

She said she was the happiest mom in Oregon when she saw me, and she may have been right. I stuffed myself with lasagna and because I can be as stupid as the next guy if I give myself half a chance, I drank red wine. With wine I usually just drink a glass, maybe two, but my aunts were pouring and my uncles were singing, and I had a bunch of stuff to not think about. Around midnight, the party broke up, and I was in my old room. A few minutes later, I was back in the TWA bathroom. All the lasagna, all the wine, everything. My misery was so loud my poor mother woke up, and she stayed with me for a few minutes before I could convince her to go back to her room.

I tried to get some sleep in the morning but my body swung from feverish to freezing to feverish, always one or the other. My mom once made me get up so she could give me new sheets. The afternoon was worse, which I wouldn't have guessed possible: delirium, shivers, sweat, and more vomiting.

"Mom, I'm a wreck, but I've got to get back to Seattle."

"You're not going anywhere." She pressed a warm washcloth on to my forehead. "I've already cleared tomorrow so I can stay home with you."

"No, mom, it's important, I've got to go."

"Honey, just think if it had happened in Wisconsin! Don't worry, I'm here."

She said I wasn't going anywhere because I wasn't in any condition to go anywhere. And nothing, she said, was more important than my health. Whatever I thought was so important would just have to wait.

I called April at three o'clock that Monday, my eyes burning as I held the phone, the receiver slippery in my feeble grip. I told her the truth: I was sicker than I'd ever been in my life, that I'd been bed-ridden and throwing up for twelve straight hours, that it showed no signs of getting better, that every medication I'd taken, over-the-counter and prescriptive, hadn't done a thing. There was diarrhea, too. Endless. Everything endless. I told her I was sorry, I was so sorry, but I wasn't going to be able to be there with her. Maybe her roommate, or the friend with the car, could go with her. I apologized again and again until she finally said "okay, okay, I understand, I really do," and "I'll see you when you're better," and then she hung up. I continued sick for two more days. I had never been, nor have been since, so physically ill.

Thursday morning, I was on the nine o'clock to Seattle. I caught a local from the station and went right to the dorm, but her roommate said she had gone home, was staying home for a few days. I called her, but she didn't want to talk much. She said she felt dead. She said her parents didn't know and it was hard not telling them. She said all she did was hurt. She said I shouldn't call her there, and that we should talk next week.

Next week arrived, and we spent another miserable day walking those same campus paths, hand in hand. She said she forgave me. If she did, she's the only one.

A Nica in Blighty

When he was learning English he craved only those past tense verbs with the full -ed syllable. English was sufficiently absurd without trying to work out the random nature of "sometimes it was '-ed' and sometimes 'just -d,'" and that was just the speaking, forgetting for a moment, if you could, which you couldn't, the variety of spelling options for a simple past tense verb: "drop the y for i, and add -ed;" or, "double the final consonant and add 'ed;'" and the laundry list of "irregular" verbs that was long enough, and bizarre enough, to send a fourteen year old boy back, screaming in the night, to Managua. But he couldn't go back, wouldn't if he could, so he refrained from the screaming-night-trip home.

English had long become second nature, a true second language, and he could spin verbs better than many natives. But in his head, alone in the mornings, he indulged himself by employing only verbs with solid "-ed" endings. He urinated. If he were in a hurry, he pee-ed. He dress-ed. He meditated. He shit-ed. He shave-ed. He open-ed the window and look-ed outside. He open-ed and close-ed the door and walk-ed to the bakery, where he ate breakfast. Even in the privacy of his mind he could not bring himself to say "eat-ed." Or "drink-ed." But those were the only two. He still felt scars from his early struggles with those two.

This day, a Wednesday, he neither meditate-ed nor shave-ed, so anxious he was to get to the station early to queue in the long *Valencia Nord* ticket lines. He had a journey that on a good day took nine hours, Valencia to Malaga, and it wouldn't do to miss the train. Beyond Malaga would be Benalmadena and Marbella, and even Gibraltar, and in each town readings and book-signings for largely ex-pat Brit audiences enchanted by his collection of essays written in Cambridge, *A Nica in Blighty.*

The later experiences in the book, age twenty-four to twenty-nine, had been the finest of his life. Jogging each morning along the Cam, gazing on sunny days from the rooftop of the old church over the lovely city, playing Saturday football on the broad green of Parker's Piece, he loved all of it. Until then paradise was barely in his vocabulary, whether Spanish—*paraiso* - or English, but he'd found it when he first stepped off the train in Cambridge, just fifty-one minutes from London's Kings Cross. And now he lived in Spain, in Valencia, which wasn't hell on earth, but neither was it paradise. But even if it were hellish at times, it wasn't Managua. Managua was a hell-realm unimagined by Dante or anyone else.

The —ed routine completed, he arrived with a generous amount of time to spare, time he loved anyway, to spend at this or any train station. The lines were shockingly short and in moments he had his ticket and an excellent people-watching perch, hot chocolate in hand, prepared to sit, to watch, to follow the vagaries of his mind.

Vagaries. The vagaries lived down the street from the Muses. In the neighborhood of publishing, *A Nica in Blighty*, printed only in soft cover with its photo of Jose Maria jaunty in a punt, just below Cambridge's version of the Bridge of Sighs, had clicked, had struck chords. It put him on all the BBC chat shows, and it paid for the Valencia flat. It wasn't *Harry Potter*, so it couldn't buy anything in Cambridge, but it sold, and sold in English far more than its Spanish version (his own translation), though fully sixty-percent of the pages were set in Nicaragua: in Bluefields, with his English-speaking cousins, in Managua (only to portray his childhood miseries), and mostly in Leon, the old capital, his grandfather's home and the site of his own awakening and transformation. The Nicaraguan pages came in at: Leon, 70%; Bluefields, 20%; and Managua with an overly-generous 10%. The book's other eighty pages were, to his mind now, typical fish-out-of-water tales set in Cambridge. The introduction itself, the bridge between the two countries, flashed a peek at his California high school and undergraduate days, when he really did have water dripping from his back.

He loved Leon. He hated Managua. He enjoyed Bluefields. California, San Francisco to be precise, he feared at first, then liked, then hated, then liked again. Cambridge? Bliss. Valencia? Not Cambridge, but soft enough.

And Valencia's *Playa Malvarossa* continued to surprise him. It was a five-minute walk from his third floor flat to the beach itself, not the prettiest in town, nor the most peaceful, but a beach that had its own life and breathed to its own rhythm. On Monday, an ordinary day, he was sitting mid-way between the waves and the cement walk, considering the late morning eastern sky, supplied with a book of Keats and a towel, when from the south he sensed two people approaching.

He opened his notebook to find Monday's words:

The man wearing the thong is walking casually in front, and sometimes to the side, but never to the rear of the woman. She wears shorts, no top, and knee pads—knee pads! - and she crawls, hands and knees, north up the beach for one-hundred-fifty meters. I look for a leash but don't see one. After ten minutes of this she rises to her feet and walks next to the man, his left arm around her shoulder. They stop, she removes her shorts and knee pads, revealing her own thong, and they continue north, the waves arriving on their right. Now they return south, each with a marvelous and superbly tanned body, cross within ten yards of me and then away from the Mediterranean, disappearing among the parked cars and construction company trucks.

I continue to sit. Did this happen?

I feel the need to abandon towel, book, and life as I used to know it, to run as if I were younger, but I know I can never catch them.

He taught two classes each semester, one in Latin American Literature, and the other, his favorite, Creative Non-Fiction, and he worked on his own novel. Next year, far too soon for sabbatical eligibility, he'd already arranged to drop the Literature course. The added liberty, plus the summer, and *"basta*, enough," the novel would declare itself and see the light.

After boarding the train and finding his seat he glanced at his pocket ARCO map, the rumble of the *"Garcia y Lorca"*–great name for a train–signaling the departure. If he had a car, he could drive it in five hours, maybe four. If he had a car and if he could drive. Either the Sierra Nevada range was bigger than he thought, or the engineer had a flock of friends and relatives scattered about, and this route was his way of keeping in touch. Xativa. Albacete. Puente Genil and Fuente de Piedra. And still not Malaga. Bobadilla before Malaga. He had no complaint, he cherished a good train ride, but the route was a curious one. He wrote, he watched, he listened, he read. It was a rolling idyll, an Eden, or perhaps Arden, on wheels. When he was a kid his grandfather, who had grown up in Mexico, often told him about that country's Copper Canyon railroad. Even before the old man began to tell the tale one more time, the memory of the experience transformed him. His face and entire body dropped twenty years. His eyes shone, his voice slowed to a crawl, idled, then raced with the once-lived scenes.

Jose Maria's first proper railroad was in the states, the Amtrak "California Zephyr" to and from Chicago. His Copper Canyon was Colorado's Glenwood Canyon. His own grandchildren, if he ever had children, if he ever found the right woman, they would see his face change in the telling.

He opened a new notebook. It was black, spiral-bound, 70 pages. On the first page he wrote:

Hoy es miércoles, el primer dia de octubre. By the end of this calendar year, I swear, I will have "getted" the right woman, and by the end of next calendar year, I will have "be-getted." It is time and estoy listo. I am ready. My life alone has ended.

And he added: *End-ed*

Always Another Straw

I've known my brother all my life but I never saw it coming. I didn't know he was going until he flat-out told me across the kitchen table, the August sun rising just a bit later than the day before. I was pouring coffee and he could have been saying: "Pass the cream," like he'd done a million times before, but instead he said:

"Rob Berryhill's giving me a ride to the station at eleven-thirty."

"What's he doing that for?"

"I'm going off to Denton."

"Denton? What do you need in Denton?"

"I believe I'm going to the college there."

And that's how I learned Larry had taken it upon himself to be a student. He was twenty-seven, seven years older than me. I did a computation and figured he'd been out of school as long as he'd been *in* school, then realized that no, that wasn't quite right. But it had been a long time.

"When's he doing that?"

"Who?" Larry could play dumb when he wanted to. "Berryhill?"

"Yeah. Berryhill."

"Eleven-thirty."

My mind latched onto the only logical response. "Well, we still have time to fish. Let's get moving."

When we parked at the lake there was just one other vehicle, Charlie Boyd's rusted camper-shell Chevy.

As we grabbed our gear I asked Larry, "What do you think of Charlie's bumper-sticker now?"

"What's he got this time, I missed it."

"It says: '*My kid fought in Iraq so yours can party in college.*'"

"Does it? Is that what I'm going to do? I'm not even sure 'party' is a verb."

"Don't look to me. That's for your professors."

"'My kid fought in Iraq, blah, blah?' What's that supposed to mean?"

"Beats me. I didn't even know Charlie had a kid."

"I don't believe he does," Larry concluded, and we dropped our lines.

We fished but it was desultory. That's not a word I often use, but that's exactly what it was. Or maybe it wasn't, because it wasn't negative at all. It is a delicious thing to greet the day with your brother beside you as the water laps at your feet. All things are possible in the morning sun, especially on a lakeshore. As I tended to do at that spot, I recalled Larry reading *The Wind in the Willows* to me during my otherwise lonely childhood.

I don't know why teachers never assigned that book in school. I understand more things each year but some things refuse explanation.

On the way back to town we stopped at the pancake place. They don't make pancakes anymore, haven't changed the sign, but Della can still fry eggs, despite losing her best waitress, her husband, and three fingers off her right hand on Fourth of July weekend.

Larry paid his respects at the counter and ordered for both of us. When he joined me in the corner booth I asked how Della was doing.

"Don't know. I asked if the highway deciding not to come this way after all was maybe the last straw for her, but she didn't say anything."

"You're sure she heard you?"

"Oh, yeah, it wasn't true about her hearing," Larry replied. "She's just tired of listening to people 'half-commiserate, half-gloat' about her old man and Irene, so she let on that she'd lost a bit in her left ear. Except for her hand, she's fine."

"You think her husband knew about the highway?"

"That's another professor question."

Della arrived with a pot of coffee and not one word. We followed her lead until she came back with our eggs, mine scrambled, his over-easy, home fries, and extra toast. Larry tried again:

"Della, are you at peace so soon?"

"Do I look like I am at peace? If I do, you both need glasses. Or in your case, Larry, a new prescription. The damn thing is she was such a good worker. She's the one I miss. Piper, if this place ever gets busy again, you've got a job if you want it."

"Thanks, Della, but I'm done with restaurant work, or any indoor stuff. I'm getting enough hours with the tree service. But I appreciate it."

Larry asked her: "What about Clark?"

"What about him? He was pretty much a zero the last few years anyway. I don't get what she sees that I didn't, but I don't guess I need to."

She left us, leaving Larry to confess what each of us remembered:

"We were sitting right here, the first day Irene came in, wearing that t-shirt that said *Not Everything in Nebraska is Flat*. I truly understood the term 'visual aid.'"

"Maybe you are ready for college."

We ate, nothing more to say. Larry grabbed the check so I got the tip. Della called out as the screen door thwacked shut behind us: "There's always another straw."

"She's developing a case of pessimism. You may be fortunate to be leaving town."

"Fortunate or not," he said, "it is time to go."

Dust chased our tires as I eased out onto the two-lane. I wondered how long Larry had known he was leaving today. I decided I didn't need to know the answer. He interrupted just as I was concluding that thought.

"I have to admit, it is hard to imagine Irene running off with Clark. She's the most gorgeous thing to ever hit this town, and Clark? Really? Irene and Clark? Hard to see."

"Didn't you always say: 'don't judge a book by its cover,' stuff like that?"

"You did listen! Mother would have been proud. I mean, I tried but I knew Irene was never going to see me as anything but a big buddy. She sure did light up a room."

"She does, she does. So what are you going to study over there anyway?"

"Does? I believe that's a present-tense verb. I was thinking Engineering, but maybe I'm a natural for English. '*Does?*' Do you know something I don't know? I mean, something in particular, aside from the multitude of things you know that I haven't a clue about."

"Can you keep a secret?"

"I'm your big brother and I can toss you across a room if I want to, so why don't you just go ahead and tell me."

"Larry, can you keep a secret?"

"Okay, yes, I can keep a secret."

"Clark and Irene did *leave* together, but he just gave her a ride to the old Drake cabin on his own way out of town. Where he is nobody knows, and if Della doesn't care, I don't think anyone else needs to either."

"You mean she's been across the lake from us all this time? What's she doing out there?"

"She's painting. And meditating. And making room for me almost every night."

"You rascal! You red-faced little punk! Damn! You and Irene. Damn!"

We walked back into the house. Larry lugged his already-packed duffel bag to the porch to be ready for Rob Berryhill and I sat down on the steps with him. We sat a minute before he laughed, repeated his "Damn! Irene! Damn!" then jumped up and ran back into his room.

He came back and plopped a book next to me. "Give her this, will you. She told me she'd never read it." It was *The Wind in the Willows*, the faded red paperback edition. "Now I know she'll love it."

"She'll get it tonight. I was going to tell you, we were going to have you out to the cabin, have a barbecue, but here you are leaving town on us."

We heard Rob's VW before we saw it. It coughed and barked but it always got people where they needed to go. Larry hugged me and whispered:

"Piper, I have to admit I'm jealous as hell, but I'll get over that. Mostly I'm thrilled for you. My baby sis is growing up."

Mobile on the 214

"Brilliant! When? Did they induce?"

Stephen Keefe folds the Guardian he has already read, has only picked up because it was on his seat as he scrambled out of the sudden summer rain onto the 214 toward Parliament Hill. He sets it down to better concentrate on the monolog in front of him though such discourses ordinarily annoy him. Easily twice each week on this very bus he imagines a swift tai chi movement, though he knows nothing of tai chi, in which he seizes and hurls a mobile out an open window. The clatter as it strikes concrete and skitters off poles, now that is a sound he could embrace. But not today. This time he warms to the words tumbling toward him (were his mother alive, she'd brand him a curtain-twitcher, but technology had changed the rules since her time). He'd picked up something from the 30-ish pink-haired girl jabbering in front of him. What had she said? Fortunately, she repeats word for word, as far as he can tell, either for emphasis or from excitement, all that she had already said.

"Just like that? At noon? It came on its own, after all? Bloody hell! After all that worrying, all those scare stories everyone told you, natural as could be!"

Natural isn't all it is cracked up to be. If Stephen knows anything, and sometimes he wonders, he knows that. He glances at the heel of his right hand, seeking the long-faded tooth marks where his wife had drawn blood, biting him so deeply as to require stitches, during "natural" childbirth. And how relieved he had been to suffer that pain, to transport him from the hollowness of standing like a scarecrow as she writhed and sweated and cried and cursed, standing with nothing to offer. Wretched with responsibility and impotency, he clutched her hand, whispered, encouraged, lied. When he winced from the atavistic cut of her teeth, he rejoiced.

"I love it. 'Henry.' That just sounds so right! You're proper parents, and I'm an auntie."

A boy. An afternoon boy, like his own son. Early on in the dank delivery room he had commented, deadpan, that he hoped "it would be over soon, because West Ham and Chelsea would be on, and it looked to be a good match." His wife knew he was joking (it had actually been her joke, originally, spoken at home before coming in to hospital), but he sensed disapproval from the attending nurse. No, "sensed" was inaccurate, too mild. The nurse fired high-caliber daggers, mixing her metaphoric weapons, but striking effectively despite her unjust verdict. Doubtless the bloody hand he received was to the nurse appropriate karma. Such a curious calling, a delivery room nurse. You might as well be in a bedroom while two people were having at it, such intimacies and fears and lies you heard. He wonders now how much they actually took in, got right or wrong, and recalled and repeated later, over tea, or in pubs, or in their own beds.

His son arrived at 1:22. Damn. It was either 1:22 or 2:21. He, so good with dates and numbers, yet endlessly caught between the two options, each, on its own, sounding perfectly correct, until he reconsidered, as he always did, and tested the other in his mind. 1:22. Yes, it was 1:22.

"Yeah, yeah, can't wait to see him. And see you guys, too. You both must be exhausted."

Stephen and his wife were dead tired for a full year. Months and months, night after night, of "sleep" that was too-little and too-lousy. Nothing was wrong, doctors and friends parroted, but no one should ever live that way. He thought of his parents, the little they had told him, and more from the stories he had read and movies he'd seen, of people going about their business during the bombing raids of their war. An entire city sleepless. How did it function? Mustn't there have been terrible decisions made, in families, in shops, in offices, in spaces packed with short-tempered, over-stressed people? He remembers the first time he had ever stayed up all night. It had been a "sleepover" at a friend's house when they were about ten. When they eventually fell asleep at five o'clock the next afternoon, he swore he never wanted that fatigue again. Ten years after, add to that the emotions and worries of an adult. Two nominal adults, that is, with an infant that neither had any idea what to do with. Two adults with increasingly little idea what to do about each other.

Serenity of a sort arrived the second year, and as the boy was approaching three, but what never returned was the zest of the pursuit, or even the passions that carried into the half year of marriage before the birth. There was no fighting. They were numb, disinterested in the other's touch, even in the other's eyes. It had no definition but it was inescapable. Inescapable until Stephen forged a route. Her name was Liz, and she was, until that time, equally close to both of them. On a weekend when his wife was away, he told Liz he was attracted to her. Years later, he realizes how foolish that statement had been, almost worse, really, than the subsequent coupling itself, which repeated itself only as required to explode his marriage. If you tell a woman, one who is already a friend, that you hold thoughts about her in that way, either action, or damage, or both, must follow. It is the kind of thing you shouldn't say unless you really know what you wanted. He believes it a universal lesson. But the action served him, for it hastened the inevitable conclusion.

His first departure, they agreed, was temporary, to give them a chance to think. He was gone four weeks, finances fortunately not a problem for them in that time, thanks to her generous and non-judging parents, living an ocean away. He took a small room on the coast, walking, reading, going alone to a cinema each Friday night no matter what the title. He returned, not sure why, to a week of false starts, strained silences, and fumbling love-making, then abruptly left again, a rail pass in his pocket. He would need to resume his own academic career soon, somewhere. On the trains he saw things he long ago should have seen. In one smoky carriage after another he realized he had made a series of bad decisions, beginning with taking on the role of "husband" when he barely felt himself a man. Perhaps some men his age could do it. He could not. Re-joining his wife would be one more such decision, and he was not going to do it.

In Norwich, on the walls of the old castle, he discovered and copied Masefield's words onto the cover of his notebook:

My road calls me, lures me
West, East, South, North,
Most roads lead men homewards,
My road leads me forth.

He rang home that night. In a long, easier than he had expected conversation, they reached an accord. When he returned to gather his belongings and resolve the minutiae, he found her more comfortable than she'd ever been in the time he'd known her. A peace was in her face, and her dealings with the boy were effortless (he knew they weren't, but compared to earlier times, so they appeared).

Their son lost the most, but waiting fifteen years would have been insane for both of them, for all three. Stephen missed the largest part of his son's boyhood and teenage years, the mother and child returning to the states, to her native Nebraska. With the boy now a man and to Stephen's good fortune working in East London, they have developed a comfortable footing. It isn't the relationship it could have been; more importantly, though, it isn't the relationship it would have been. His wife had re-married, not right away, but successfully, and with the good services of distance and time, she and Stephen had created a state of fond friendship. Stephen failed again at a marriage, having learned too little too soon, but now he could claim to be in a long-standing mature (he dared use that term) relationship. Each keeps a flat on opposite sides of the Heath, she near Queens Park, he, on Swains Lane, and each intends to maintain the refuge, but they thoroughly delight in and appreciate what they have, and reasonably believe they will enjoy each other for the rest of their years.

The 214 halts suddenly, at his stop, his body recognizing it prior to his consciousness, the mobile and its owner long silent, long departed. He nods to the driver and steps down, and as he does so he smiles at the familiar courtship sounds from the teenagers in the park shadows. He quickly crosses Highgate and strides the short distance to his door, keys jangling and telephone numbers rattling in his head, the August evening skies clear again. The clock in his favor, he will ring his son's mother in Omaha to thank her one more time. He will see Josh next week, their regular second Tuesday of the month, so he doesn't really need to push his number, but he will anyway. Then he will ring Anne. Just to talk, their words arcing across the heath, lips to ear and back again, keeping the lines open.

River Walk in a Railroad Town

My grandmother once told me that until she was eight years old, she had an older sister. We were walking the river after services on a fall Sunday morning, and I can only guess it came up because I mentioned that I wished I had a sister. I remember saying I'd even settle for a brother.

I don't know what I expected, but without preamble, without even a change in her voice, she said: "My sister was fourteen. She was skinny as a rail but she was strong. She worked so hard my folks didn't need to hire any help except at harvest time."

I prided myself as the family historian and could recite the grandparents on both sides, including birthdates, plus the aunts and uncles and cousins and shirttail relatives. I'd always known her to be an only child, as I was. I was following her path, and my mother's path: the lone child, the only daughter.

We stopped near the pier and sat on the Armistice Day bench. It was built last year, seven Novembers since the end of the Great War.

"I didn't know you had a sister."

She didn't say anything more and I followed her eyes as she watched a black and green tugboat nudging a coal barge north. It was making slow progress.

I waited. I resisted pulling out my little notepad from my handbag. If she said anything more, I wanted to remember.

"This was a long time ago, of course. We lived so far out in the country and we didn't come to town more than once a month."

"You grew up near Yarmouth, right? It's still such a tiny town."

"That's right, Sweetie, we were a little north of there, and it wasn't any bigger even then. We raised corn, fruit trees, and dust. It was not easy."

As a high school student, I was smart enough, or educated enough, to know my childhood was easier than hers had been. Everyone in town had electricity and half had indoor plumbing. Six families had automobiles. We had a hospital and a school. Nothing of that was available to her when she was growing up. I also knew that at fifteen it was unlikely I'd ever have a sister or a brother.

"So, one morning, a steaming August day just after my birthday, my sister Abigail came running from the west fields, hollering to beat the band. I was standing on the porch with my mother. We heard her before we saw her."

"What happened?" I asked.

"Her face and arms were bloody. At first, she couldn't tell us anything, but at some point she was able to put words together. She said it was a fox."

"Foxes usually avoid people," I said, stupidly.

"This one didn't, and the next few weeks were terrible. Abigail screamed and flinched anytime we tried to touch her. I'd never seen her afraid before, but she'd changed into a new being. The cuts turned to scars and she picked at them and ripped open the sores. Even after she stopped scratching, something ate from the inside. We didn't know what it was and she wouldn't talk to any of us. That was the hardest part for me.

"Please don't misunderstand me, because I felt horrible for her– we all did–but her silence fell hardest on me. She was my only companion. I was the little sister who looked up to her big sister, but I also knew that her pain was far worse for her than for me. I knew that, and yet half of my own crying at night was for me."

Grandmother stopped again. She stared across the water as if she had locked on to something on the other side, something only she could see. "This went on for a month and just when I thought she was starting to come around, everything fell apart," she said. "I woke up in the room we shared and she was drooling. She was fourteen years old and drool slid down her chin. Then, her body shook like that St. Vitus Dance people talk about. She couldn't control it. That's when we knew, or when my parents knew, anyway. I didn't understand until later."

"What was wrong with her?" I said.

"The fox was rabid."

49

"We learned about rabies in school, in Science class, and about Louis Pasteur." Again I urged myself to be quiet.

She rose and I followed, and we walked further north as The Mississippi rolled south toward Missouri.

Grandmother looked at me and said, "Yes, but in those days there was no treatment, no cure."

"What do you mean no cure?"

"Exactly that. The first bite doomed her. She had nothing but horrible days ahead. All we could do was hope for the mercy of death."

"What did you do? What did the doctors do?"

"Sweetheart, there was nothing a doctor could do, or anyone else. Each day was worse than the day before. One night, after a long week of this, my father took her out of the house. He carried her into the barn and strangled her."

My arms and legs trembled. I grabbed grandmother's hands.

"It was three hours, maybe four, before he came back inside and told Mother and me what he'd done, but I already knew. I had followed them and slipped into the barn from the other side. I was in the shadows where we stacked the hay. He never saw me hiding."

I had hugged my grandmother often, but when we collapsed into each other's arms, I knew I would never forget that embrace. And I haven't.

We walked up Division Street. It was time for supper.

When we climbed the steps and entered our house, my parents were already seated. My grandmother sat beside my mother. People always told me I looked like them but I never saw it. I started to sit but I stopped, went to the corner of the parlor, pulled a fifth chair up to the table, and placed it between my grandmother and me.

I never did have a sister but we had that chair.

Always Present, Always Watching

Kenny didn't need a book, didn't want a book, had no business being in Dog Eared Books on Valencia Street except that's where they'd said they'd meet, so they could walk together to the marriage counselor's office. Tuesdays had become, they joked without laughing, date night. Fifty minutes with Dr. Cortes–"call me Alicia"–followed by dinner somewhere in the Mission, followed by a kiss on the cheek before his wife hopped on the BART to Berkeley and her new apartment and he walked home alone. He found little to say to Alicia, despite or perhaps because of her gentle questions, but he had agreed to try the counseling so he kept coming.

But he didn't need a book. He had one in his bag right now, not to mention five or six on his bedside table. He was browsing the new releases when he noticed a familiar name beneath an unfamiliar title. The author was LaDonna Alton, a name he hadn't thought of in over twenty years. He was forty-five now, so he'd gone half his life and more since the last time.

He picked up the paperback and read the jacket:

Sardonic, sarcastic and often flat-out sensual, Alton's debut
story collection offers a delicious set of coming-of-age, coming-through,
and even coming-out stories. Women, and the men and women who
love them, will find themselves here, or wish that they were.

He looked at the small author photo inside. He had no doubt that it was "his" LaDonna Alton. The decades had been kind to her, not that she'd needed any help.

The day they met he was working at Del's Drugs in Flagstaff and she and her mom had just moved in to the two-story apartment building down the block from the store.

"Where do you keep the female products?"

It was only his second week of work and though he had a mother and an older sister, at age sixteen the words embarrassed him. He swiped the counter with a rag as he tried to recover his communication skills.

"Over there," he said, "against that wall under the clock."

He watched as she followed his words and pointed finger. She had brown hair that curled on the sides but was tied in a short ponytail that bounced as she walked toward the display case. Her body was a little round–not fat, but maybe plump, though he never did know exactly what "plump" meant. Perhaps chunky was a better call, but he wasn't sure. She was slightly wider around the hips than a lot of girls he knew, and she was probably 5'2 or 5'3, an important consideration as he was barely 5'5.

A few moments later she returned to his register with two different boxes of tampons, a tube of Colgate toothpaste, two toothbrushes and a bar of soap. She put them on the counter, said "Wait a sec," and headed to the same aisle. This time she came back with a bottle of Prell shampoo and two rolls of toilet paper.

"We had to leave Phoenix a little fast."

He thought about girls with each in-breath but he hadn't known exactly what, or who, he was looking for until he stared into her face. Mixed messages from art classes and pop songs and *Playboy* magazines flooded his vision, and try as he might to objectively take her whole self in, he was fixated on her lips. He'd not yet kissed a girl but now he understood why that had to change. It looked like someone–Van Gogh? Michelangelo? God?–had painted a rose, or a peach, or both somehow, and transformed them into lips.

"Excuse me. Do you want to ring me up?" She pointed at the stuff.

"Oh, yeah. I'm sorry." He skillfully priced and bagged the purchases while he inhaled greenish-brown eyes, a freckled nose, and the cheekbones that carried the slightest constellation of acne.

It took a while but they became real friends. She and her mom had landed in Flagstaff after leaving, under cover of night, a man who preferred greyhound racing and bouts of whiskeys and beer to the staid life of marriage and fatherhood. Kenny had never pressed for details and LaDonna hadn't offered. He'd always felt that she didn't want him to ask about all that.

By spring semester of junior year, after the snow stopped falling and had melted away, they often held hands as they walked alongside the railroad tracks, but only if they were sure her mom was miles away. Sometimes they hiked on the trails in the foothills of the majestic San Francisco Peaks. At 12,000 feet, they were snow-capped year round. Flagstaff was his home the first twenty-four years of his life and he would never tire of those mountains. They were protectors.

That year, 1985, once again someone had the bright idea to turn the Peaks into a "world-class ski resort" to rival Aspen, Tahoe and Vail, but once again a determined coalition of environmental and tribal forces prevented it. Those particular peaks were not only pristine, they were sacred to the Navajo and to the Hopi, and to Kenny.

Looking up at them from town, hiking below them in the summers, or drawing and painting them in art class, they were the closest Kenny ever came to religion. He loved taking her up the trails, showing her the different views, explaining–she called him "Professor" when he got carried away, but always with a smile–about the native species, the growths within growths, the variety of the critters.

LaDonna and her mom were Nazarene, a brand of faith of which he knew nothing. He had seen the church, on Soliere Avenue near the highway, but that's all. His own parents had been Catholic but hadn't really passed it on to him, and when his dad asked for and got a divorce from his mom when he was nine, his mom abandoned the whole idea. The only time he was anywhere near a church, Catholic or otherwise, was when he played basketball in the Catholic Youth Organization (CYO) leagues. He was always short and scrawny, but he compensated, as his coaches reminded him, by also being slow. Still, he loved to play, and his teammates came from across the community: Catholics, Baptists, Nothings, Whites, Mexicans, and Indians. Even Cowboys from ranches just out of the city. It was years later that he realized how very *catholic* the whole thing had been, and hooray for the CYO.

"We can't dance," she told him when he asked her to the Prom.

"Who can't? You and me?"

"No, silly, Nazarenes. Nazarenes can't dance. I'm not even supposed to hold hands but I tell myself it's like we're little kids. It was okay back then."

They waited for a lumbering freight train before crossing the tracks to walk south, away from town and toward the college campus.

"Doesn't look good for my chances, then," he said.

She squeezed his hand and looked at him.

"I mean," he said, "with you. You know, like girlfriend? Boyfriend?"

"Oh, Kenneth." Except for his dead grandmother, no one other than LaDonna had ever called him that. He was Kenny, and sometimes Ken, to the entire living world. Had been, until she came to town.

She continued: "Even if we weren't Nazarene, I'm not ready for any of that, and you really know that, don't you? You truly understand me."

They were now far enough from town to hold hands, so they did. He thought about what she'd said. She was right, he did know her, probably better than he knew himself. Even though he'd fantasized about being her boyfriend, and he was a skilled fantasizer–he had the stained sheets to prove it–he had known it wasn't going to happen, and that they'd be friends with a small "f" for as far into the future as either one of them could imagine. Even if she had said yes to the prom invitation, the overall picture would not have changed.

Prom came and went and the closest he got was hearing about it in the cafeteria the next week, and then two weeks later looking at unending collections of stiffly-posed photographs, and presto, it was summer.

He got more hours at the drugstore and LaDonna got a job at a new child-care center but she had to quit after a week. She said her mom said some preacher, not their local one, maybe one on television, had announced that women who left their kids in day care were as sinful as those who had abortions. That was the end of that.

Her apartment building had a swimming pool–he didn't know many people who had one–and she was allowed to swim in it with him present, which surprised and delighted him. For a moment he thought she must be lying about getting her mom's permission but he chased the thought away. She did not lie. She even wore a real swimsuit but it was no bikini. Four or five bikinis could have been made out of the purple material that made up her one-piece, maybe ten, but he wasn't complaining. There was enough visible skin to make him happy at the pool, and later, excited at home in bed. For some reason few of the other residents ever used the pool, and when they did it was usually really early in the morning or late in the afternoon; as a result, LaDonna and Kenny had the place to themselves most mid-days if he wasn't working. She told him that her neighbors were "pretty old," and that she was the only teen in the building.

On the Fourth of July, a day the drugstore was closed, she called to invite him over, "and there's someone I want you to meet!"

He said he'd be there by noon. He stopped at the Circle K for a bag of chips and a big bottle of A&W Root Beer. When he arrived at the complex he trotted around to the back and hopped the little fence that surrounded the pool area. She was sitting on the side with her legs dangling in the water. Maybe she wasn't his girlfriend but he could look, and he did. He put his stuff on the umbrella-shaded table and slipped out of his sandals and torn *Ghostbusters* t-shirt. He was already wearing cut-offs, the only swimming apparel he owned. As he turned back to her someone surfaced in the deep end and it was not one of the neighbors.

"Joely. Joely! He's here!" LaDonna's valiant effort seemed to fail because the swimmer returned to the blue depths beneath the diving board, but within moments the body–Joely, presumably–reached the metal ladder next to LaDonna and pulled itself out.

This new girl had brown hair that looked black because it was so wet, and the hair was long, ending far below her shoulders. She was

55

skinny—that was the only word for it—and she barely showed anything beneath her own suit. This suit was a two-piece—"skimpy," that was a good word—with tiny white stars dancing on the shiny, satin-like red material.

Their relationship was never clear. It was something indirect like shirttail cousin or stepsister-once-removed. Joely was eighteen, two years older than they were, and was to be in town for just three or four days. The next day, at the pool, he was kissing her. He was kissing a real girl. It only happened in the pool, and only in the daytime, and only with LaDonna in attendance, either sitting on the edge or in a chair under the umbrella. Always present, always watching.

With the first kiss he closed his eyes like guys did in the movies. They stayed shut even when Joely's tongue poked into his mouth; however, when she put his right hand on top of her left breast, he shivered, and he opened his eyes and looked straight at LaDonna. His eyes remained open for every kiss that day, never straying from LaDonna's face.

The day after that, Joely slid his hand *under* her top. At first he didn't move it at all, afraid to break the spell, barely believing it was happening, but she whispered a bit of instruction and soon he was gently flicking with his fingers and feeling a hardened nipple.

"I'm leaving the day after tomorrow, you guys," Joely confirmed as they all toweled off beside the pool. The girls went up to the apartment and Kenny went home to change clothes before his shift at the drug store.

On the final day at the pool, with LaDonna sitting across from them in her usual spot at the ladder, Joely slipped his hand between her legs as if the bikini bottom didn't exist. He touched wet hair and soft skin and then his fingers were guided, first up and down, and then, gently, inside, as she shuddered into his ear. He kept his hand where she wanted it and he kept his eyes on LaDonna, who watched him.

As promised, Joely disappeared, taking the bus to Amarillo. Summer meandered in her wake and neither wanted to talk about those four days. They spoke of everything else: their classes for senior

56

year, Little Bear Trail on the mountain, favorite flowers, and the customers he saw at work. They walked and walked and if they were far enough across the tracks or in the hills, they held hands.

Just before Labor Day, with no warning to Kenny, her father showed up and whisked mom and daughter away. It happened so fast that he found out only via a phone call from the apartment, the last call before the service was cut off and the U-Haul headed for parts unknown.

Two months into senior year Kenny pulled a postcard from his mailbox with a photo of *"World Famous Wall Drug, South Dakota."* The message read: *Saw this and thought of you. It's just Mom and me again and that's good. Keep your eyes open. LaDonna*

Twenty-plus years later he was a grown-up and a husband and an ecologist for a large land trust. He was an excellent ecologist, an adequate adult, and a failing husband. His wife had initiated the separation and neither had any true expectation they would reconcile. The counseling was designed to ease the transition.

He carried the book to a stuffed chair in a back corner. He was sure he would buy it but he wanted to sit with it for a while. He marveled at the clarity available from some, but not all, memories. He had recently heard, though he could not recall where he'd been, a new-to-him connotation of the word "remember" as more like "re-member," as in putting things back together, or returning to what once had been.

He rose again and took the book to the register, paid the $12.95 and tax and slid *Poolside and Other Stories* into his bag. He walked into the cool San Francisco air to wait for his wife. He wondered what was waiting for him, both in the book and on the therapist's couch, for tonight he had something to say.

Funeral Season

First there were only six, and then a few more arrived before noon, but the room was far from full. Nils wasn't shocked at the low turnout but he was disappointed and that surprised him. He had attended so many funerals in the past year, almost always with Tommy at his side. At the last two he had gone alone because Tommy was too weak. Today was his lover's turn.

The hospice people had instructed him regarding the morphine. He knew what Tommy had wanted and what he didn't want and the last couple of days the one gift he could offer was the morphine, drip by drip by drip.

Tommy had been the one to declare, sometime in the last twelve or eighteen months, that the smart money was always in death and that if he had some money to invest he'd put it all in the mortuary market. "Or maybe caskets." He had even suggested, late one night, that they walk together the next morning to the high school where he taught English, to propose to the principal that the school form a teenage pallbearer drill-team. Think of it, wearing their school green and gold, marching in step, another dead man on their shoulders, good for school spirit, no? Well, no, probably, it wouldn't be, and they never did approach the principal. Tommy had loved his classroom since he had started teaching in the early sixties, but as his strength slipped and then slipped beyond that, he'd been placed on an extended "district medical leave" that looked a lot like early retirement, also known as retirement-just-in-time-for-death. It was not what Tommy had imagined, Nils knew, and it certainly wasn't what they had planned as a couple.

Nils and Tommy had been together since 1968. They had almost reached their platinum anniversary, not that the law would agree, but even if it did, "almost," as Tommy had often told his students, almost was worth less than an empty album jacket, even if the album cover proclaimed Bob Dylan or David Bowie. Close to twenty years but no cigar, no platinum.

There were no rock and roll churches in San Francisco so Tommy had chosen the next best thing, the *Church of John Coltrane*, at the corner of Fillmore and Eddy. The congregation was primarily African-American and Tommy was even whiter than Wisconsin-born Nils, but it had always been a welcoming place and had been their Sunday sanctuary for several years. Tommy did have jazz albums but their number paled when compared to his rock collection. He had it all, from the early days of Bo Diddley and Bill Haley and Buddy Holly, to the mellow eighties of Fleetwood Mac and Van Morrison. Van Morrison dominated their stereo these days.

Irony was an important word in Tommy's English classes and at home, too, and Nils often heard, *had* heard, he knew he must begin to say, the oddity of the remarkable lack of anger in the modern music scene. This at a time when people were dying left, right and center to this plague upon homosexual men in San Francisco and New York and plenty of heartland points in between. Where were the angry young men? Oh.

The preacher spoke appropriate but well-worn words and then Nils took the unnecessary microphone. *Funeral fatigue*, he'd seen it written, and that was a fair phrase.

"I turned fifty-five last week. Tommy was barely fifty. I've been poring through my books for guidance, for comfort, for anything that might help get me, get us, through this hell. Auden. Keats. Ferlinghetti. Plath. Woolf. Whitman. I don't know what I was hoping to find. I just know that I didn't find it. And I know that I've come to detest the word 'hope.'

Forgive me, Father, but there's a word I keep seeing on 24th Street over in the Mission District–*precita*–such a lovely word and yet, and I do speak and understand some Spanish, only recently did I learn that *precita* means *damned*, it means condemned to Hell. That's what it feels like sometimes in the city. Tommy's awful dying was a hell realm for both of us and I know we're not the first to experience it.

This is the best I can do. It didn't come from the bookshelf. It didn't even come from one of Tommy's albums. It's from one of my

59

notebooks from a million years ago, when I lived in Wisconsin, when I had never been west of the Mississippi. I don't recall the occasion but maybe it was waiting for today:

Every day an anniversary
Each breath a marker
His smile in the morning
All the way to the end

There is Ezra Pound, too, though he may have been the translator, not the writer:

And the days are not full enough
And the days are not full enough
And life slips by like a field mouse
Not shaking the grass

Thank you for being here. Be well."

One tired week later, Nils sat at the kitchen table at mid-day. The apartment, once so cozily cramped, was large and empty, a shell of itself. Yes, the furniture had not changed, and yes, all Tommy's albums remained. In truth, the sole material difference was that his clothes had been donated and his toiletries and stunning array of medicines tossed in the trash. What did "larger than life" mean, Nils wondered. He had always thought it trite but the absence of Tommy was so much more than his mere corporeal self, and that self had been dissipating for months anyway. No, there was a palpable vacuum. He didn't like that term anymore than he did "larger than life." Language. Life. Shit.

Son of a Father

"Elusive as an alley cat." She was a woman I met one time only, when I was sixteen, and that's what she said, her grey eyes never lighting on me, but fixed on one dusty square of her kitchen window as she reminisced about my father, a man I had never met at all, a man she hadn't seen in twenty years. Her name was Marisol and she had once possibly been married to my mother's older brother, the one who repaired televisions and died and had a funeral when I was about five years old. I remember the funeral but not the man. Straining for the right words, her best appraisal was that my father was as elusive as an alley cat. Two decades later, I found a poem by Francisco X. Alarcon and the very phrase in Spanish: *huidizo como gato de barrio*. I was confident Sr. Alarcon was not a plagiarist, but I couldn't work out if the dates added up. I didn't think it likely she could have read it before we met. It must have been "simply"–that absurd word we use for the wrinkles of life and language–an expression from her collection.

I was *in utero* when my father went south. For longer than you might imagine it didn't cross my mind that he existed, or had existed. I didn't know his name until I was eleven–one morning a new teacher insisted I be able to write it on a family tree. Five years later, from my "aunt"–"just call me Marisol"–she must have been all of forty, and when I think back, she was an extremely attractive forty–who determinedly didn't smoke while I drank lemonade and had three of my own in her spare, spotless kitchen, in San Francisco's Sunset District in a house with no visible ashtrays, but whom I'd bet ten to one had herself smoked from the age of fourteen, and no doubt still had a stash of Camels tucked inside her sweater drawer,–I learned he wasn't the first in the family to go south, that his own father had made it all the way to the equator, the years he "worked on the canal."

Some time after our sole encounter, when she must have known she was dying, she packaged a small box of letters and photos and mailed it to me, signing the note *Aunt M.* The photos convinced me that my nose was less unique than my schoolyard friends had always imagined, and one of the letters made it clear that my grandfather (another man I never met) had once earned his keep in Panama playing piano for one of the flophouses that dotted the Isthmian Canal Commission's construction sites. Most were shacks or tents with nothing more than cots, but his, with a carefully-lettered "Smiley's," on the door, was a building of adobe brick with real beds and real women, and a bar, a piano, and my grandfather. Maybe I did have a musical bone in my body.

It was a week after I'd received the package that I realized there was a two-by-three photo I hadn't noticed, stuck to the inside of one of the envelopes. I thought it was my mom, much younger, with my dad. I thought it was, but then I knew it had to be Marisol. She was smoking and wearing a strapless summer dress. My father stood behind her, his arms around her and his hands crossing and cupping her breasts. She was looking up at his dazzling camera-ready smile. Over their heads was the clock I'd seen above her kitchen sink.

I was born in 1945, three weeks after my father bolted from a Texas army hospital. He was recuperating from a head injury he'd received overseas, or not overseas. He left prior to his medical discharge because he had it on good authority, my mother would have read in the letter he sent her and that, improbably, she saved for me, or, more likely, inadvertently neglected to destroy, for there was little else in her meager possessions to suggest she had once lived with, married, borne a child by, this man, that he had it on good authority, he was *confident,* that he could find and befriend the mysterious author— American? German? Mexican? More than one man?—who used the name B. Traven, and who was reputedly tucked away somewhere in Mexico.

To say that "I was born" is so boring. In Mexico, the expression is *dar a luz*—give the light—or, in the sense of "When is the baby due? *¿Cuando das a luz?*" But when I received the light, it wasn't enough to lay eyes on him.

The source that was the imprimatur of my father's decision was a man named Hans, a loquacious prisoner-of-war happily emptying bedpans in the hospital in San Antonio, thriving in a job much calmer than his infantry work back home. Hans confided to my father, according to the first letter, scrawled as he bounced in a southbound Mexican bus out of Nuevo Laredo, that while he had never met the man himself, his own brother-in-law, not terribly lamentably killed in '42, was once a confidante of B. Traven, and, yes, Traven was German, though that wasn't his real name. Moreover, Hans had read, after the brother-in-law passed, his packet of Traven's letters, preserved in their envelopes covered with Mexican stamps. And upon each envelope was a return address. One even had a reference to *The Treasure of the Sierra Madre*. There were six envelopes, the postmark dates not always distinct, with four different addresses. Hans recalled two of the addresses, the two which had been, he believed, the most recent, and he generously bestowed those addresses upon my father. "You are a man who will appreciate this. It is a burden I am lifting from myself."

My father had signed up in homage to Hemingway with the ambulance corps, my aunt had said, but never, she firmly believed, never crossed the ocean, for some reason serving our nation best along the Texas border. His injury, a serious one, occurred outside a roadhouse in West Texas. Or perhaps on a shooting range in San Antonio. My minimal extended family thrived in a region of selective recall.

It was from a friend of my mother that I learned something else: One afternoon before I could walk, two men from the government knocked on our apartment door in Oakland to tell her that her husband's body had been identified in a morgue in Oaxaca, Mexico.

When you seek one world, physics demands you leave another behind. Physics admits no half-measures. Here, or there, but not both. I already knew that, and a bachelor's degree-worth of other things, too, when I finally crossed the border myself, took the series of bus rides that would culminate in Oaxaca. Long miles and long hours, but you don't go forth without a reason, either a better view ahead or a worse one behind. My own rear-view mirror wasn't the worst in the world, but I would not mourn its passing. And more, south and east led to, might lead to, my father, gone since before we met, dead as long as I had been alive.

There was a man in Oaxaca who knew a family in Santa Maria del Tule who maybe knew my father. I thought I spoke and understood Spanish but I thought a lot of other things that proved to be incorrect, too. Sergio Padilla Flores and I took the bus from Oaxaca to *Tule*, its more common name, five days after my arrival. I thought Sergio was at least seventy, yet he was describing, as well as I could understand, the two brothers in Tule as a generation older. My second morning in Oaxaca, he had taken me into a double-locked storeroom in a crumbling once-proud building on La Calle Armenta y Lopez, just east of the Zocalo in the center of the city. He convinced someone to spring the locks for us. We entered a windowless area, stifling hot, packed with wood, metal, and cardboard file cabinets. Sometime during the fourth afternoon we found the newspaper from 1946. My father was one of twelve persons killed when a bus jumped the road near San Bartolo Coyotepec. The driver was one of the fatalities but three survivors spoke of a massive pack of coyotes filling the lanes as the bus began a blind descent. They surmised the coyote explosion caused the driver to react instinctively, and incorrectly, and down the bus tumbled. In an extremely rare occurrence for the time, an autopsy was performed on the driver, and his cause of death was not the crash but a heart attack.

Before I had come down, I spent four Mondays in the old San Francisco Public Library but found nothing connecting Traven to Oaxaca. That didn't worry me because everything I did read on Traven had the taste of "well, we don't really know anything concrete about this man, but we'll repeat these reports that might be true."

That last letter my mom had received, or, more properly, of the three letters in the bottom of her dresser, the one with the most recent date, was postmarked Mexico City, and suggested he was close to his quarry. Then there was a yellowed telegram from Oaxaca, inexpensive, four words: *Paydirt. Manuscript to follow.* Then nothing, nothing saved anyway, and then the knock on the door, according to the only friend I knew my mother to have, and they showed little intimacy in the time I knew them, and the news of his death.

I don't know how newspapers are preserved in the States. I am not a trained historian. I planned to be a physical therapist but after graduation never took the state boards. I have no expertise to compare this twenty-year old edition of *La Imparcial* with any other aged newspaper. I can say that compared to the March 16th San Francisco Chronicle that I half-read on the first bus, from Oakland to Los Angeles, this one was brittle. Delicate. Cradling its pages in my hands was a blessing, a gift I wanted to have earned but felt unsure that I had. The top half of the front page was a picture that looked like a still from a movie set, a close-up of two bodies propped next to the wreck of the bus, as bloody as a black and white photo can be. I didn't think either of the bodies was my father, although the face of the man on the left didn't look like any father who had ever walked this earth.

Again I wondered what the Oaxaca connection was, and it was for this question that Sergio and I were side-by-side on the Tule bus, the morning sun staring at us through the windshield, the driver's transistor radio blaring as if it knew it were chosen from all the radios in all the buses this day to represent the heart of 1966 Mexican pop music.

We reached Tule and the big tree that the guidebooks brag about, the only reason I had ever heard for visiting the town. As wide as a house and several times as tall, it is no ordinary tree. Were I a believer in alien visitations I would have thought it delivered from another galaxy. Equally captivating was the brilliant white church just behind it. Alone, it would have been a good-sized structure, but here it was dwarfed by the tree. Sergio took me into the church as soon as we were off the bus and, after doing what all good Catholics do in that part of the world, he disappeared into a side room, leaving me to gaze alone at the etchings and paintings. He returned in thirty minutes to find me on a wooden bench contemplating the suffering face of Jesus. He started to speak but paused, giving me time to re-acquaint myself with the twentieth century.

"Sr. Eduardo, I am sorry to tell you that the two gentlemen we have come to see are no longer living." This was spoken in Spanish but I had no trouble with either the literal or broader significance of the words. He continued:

"The elder brother, Don Pedro, suffered a stroke and died after a day. His younger brother, Don Miguel, hearing the news, responded with a killing stroke of his own. The masses were given this morning. Would you like to visit the cemetery?"

I looked back at Jesus on the cross. I wasn't Catholic, wasn't anything, but wished that I were.

"Yes, let's go."

It was a short walk in the relentless heat. Several mourners were leaving, though not all. A priest accompanied them. Sergio spoke softly with the priest, nodded discretely toward me, then returned to my side as the priest and the others continued their exodus.

"Over in the corner, near the bougainvillea," he told me.

The priest returned briefly. I wondered if there were more to the ceremony. In my cautious Spanish I asked him if anything else was going to happen, as I noticed many of the mourners still in the area, sitting on dusty monuments, chatting and fanning themselves. He replied that it might rain.

We walked on and easily found the freshly turned dirt and the two shiny stones: Pedro Mendez Huerta and Miguel Mendez Huerta, both awash in flowers. They were in a row of three, the third much older, the lettering less obvious. I read the name Gerard Gales. It was the same name as my father. There was nothing to say. There was no reason to be there.

A week later I was back in California reading Traven's *The Cotton Pickers* for the fifth and final time. I finished it and burned it in a metal trashcan behind my apartment building. Next I burned my father's letters. As the afternoon sun faded into an unseasonably chilly sunset, I burned the photos one by one, saving until the end the glimpse of my father, and his hands, and Marisol, not before admiring for one last time the look on her face, the smile on his, and, yes, her body, covered though it was by those hands. Then I added my passport and stoked the flames until there was nothing but ash.

I moved across the bay to San Francisco to an even worse apartment not two blocks from the corner where Marisol's kitchen and apartment had stood before falling to a wrecking ball and, in succession, a Rexall pharmacy, a real estate office, a Filipino market, and a Salvadoran restaurant.

I apprenticed for six months before signing on as a landscape gardener trainee for the city of San Francisco. I spend my days on my knees in Golden Gate Park, ripping out invasive species, replacing them with boring but native varieties as tourists step around me as if I were inanimate.

Muni runs a bus but I have had enough of buses, so each dawn I walk the two miles to the park and at dusk I walk the two miles home. My evenings are a tight circuit of three bars in the Avenues between Rivera and Taraval Streets and my nights, sleeping or not, in my cell of an apartment on 43rd Avenue. On windless nights I can't help hearing the waves from Ocean Beach but that's as close as I get to the saltwater that kisses the city's edge. I stopped reading altogether and I never think about my father.

What the Storm Brought

January was the month of truth but some truths were harder than others. The first month of 1914 had already been a challenge and then the blizzard arrived. The seventy-one citizens were as prepared as possible, had felt it coming, anticipated it even, much like the arrival of a traveling circus. No one left town for a week, not for work or for school.

Hazel had never been out of Iowa. Twice she had ventured as far as Burlington, where her father had been raised, and which was packed with hills and churches. Yarmouth had no hill and one church, and her father was the Pastor.

On ordinary frigid mornings, fourteen-year old Hazel and her thirteen-year old brother Elvin, because they'd outgrown the local schoolhouse, rode a wagon to the consolidated school south of town. To ease the journey, Papa pulled a brick out of the fire, wrapped it in a horse blanket, and stowed the bundle under the buggy's bench. And reminded Hazel: "Don't drink water!" It was six bumpy miles but Papa required that they walk the last mile. A railroad track angled across the road at that point, running northeast and southwest, and he lost sleep imagining the horse spooking at the explosion of a locomotive. Trains ran the line infrequently but Papa had sworn to his wife as she faded from them, from him, that their two children would be both protected and educated. Since her passing four years prior he had kept his promise. For the school journey, he'd arranged that they tie-up at a friend's barn and walk the final mile. If a powerful storm did catch them, Hazel and Elvin passed the night at the friend's, but that was rare.

Four days after the blizzard's worst, when they could be outside for more than thirty minutes, her brother spotted two figures making halting progress from the east, from the same railroad line that skirted the town.

"Go get Pa," Elvin ordered his older sister, before he mushed toward the specters as quickly as the heavy drifts allowed.

Hazel burst into a room little warmer than outdoors to find her father at his dark wooden desk, writing his words for the following Sunday.

Responding to her sputtering and waving, he hurried into his boots and greatcoat and into the brilliant sunlight. After repeated blinks he located the two strangers, and almost upon them, his remarkably broad-backed Elvin, and he hurried forward. He called back: "Put a kettle on, and cheese and bread!"

Back in the house, actually the parsonage that attached to the spare, square white church, Hazel surprised herself with a gasp that she'd been holding since Elvin's command. She deviated from her father's direction only by heating last night's soup before beginning to break chunks of cheese for the table. She stared from the window as the four figures trudged toward sanctuary. She willed the soup to hurry.

Now the men were sitting at the table.

Watching the ice crack and melt from their moustaches, and in the older man's case, his thick red beard, Hazel gleaned that they were indeed railroad men, a two-man crew deadheading an empty freight car over to Muscatine. "We just stopped, shook a little to the left, but it was a gentle shake, and then we were stuck," said the older man. "We were rolling well, no more than two miles from this splendid kitchen." The men had washed up a bit and were already breathing easier, looking almost relaxed in front of her. Forty-four hours had been their limit, wood and coal burned, food gone, only snow to consume. The older—he may have been twenty-five—claimed it to be "the highest *and* thickest drift" he ever had the pleasure of meeting. The younger said nothing, but when Hazel stole a glance at him as she served the soup, he held her gaze. His eyes were a shade of blue completely new to her.

The bearded man continued to speak: "That sun's a godsend, but it'll take a lot of melting and a lot of digging to clear the track. I expect they're sending a crew down to find us, and more important to them, salvage the car."

Hazel's papa told them that the storm had been said to freeze the entire valley, and likely nothing would move on the tracks anytime soon. They were welcome to take refuge with them, and they'd be "fools," he added, if they refused.

Hazel watched the young man bring the spoon to his lips.

"That'd be a blessing indeed," the older man responded, his shiver finally stilled. "My name's Larsen. Nils Larsen. This young fellow is Albert Drinkwater." Hazel's face flushed at the name. And not just for that. In the days following, Elvin and the two other strongest Yarmouth boys, his friends Earl and Major, helped clear the tracks. Elvin's energy impressed not just the two railroad men but also the crew chief from the north. Three days later, when the engine resumed its journey, Elvin was on it, abandoning father, sister, and school for a promised job in the Beloit railroad yard, all the way in Wisconsin. She had not once spoken with, nor even heard the voice of, the man called Albert.

During the year that her brother was in Beloit and she still in Yarmouth, Hazel wrote him one letter each month. In response, Elvin mailed a total of three postcards.

One Saturday in October, after Hazel had taken her morning stroll, she returned to find her father dead at his desk. With the help of neighbors she did everything that was necessary; in fact, the first few days were the easiest because it was clear what was to be done. In her letter to Elvin she wrote:

> *He was in apparent good health the day previous and with no thought of being called so suddenly from the world. Doctor Unterkircher's examination showed he died of apoplexy.*

> *Reverend Cullen came in from Mediapolis, and delivered the funeral sermon from the text from St. Paul: "I have fought a good fight, I have finished my course, I have kept the faith."*

The church allowed her to remain in the house because no new minister would be brought in. Instead, Reverend Cullen visited twice a month.

Six months after the funeral she realized she had no reason to stay, and she was already the oldest student in her school. She distributed her father's belongings to the poor and to others and closed the house. After a last day in Burlington walking the shops of Jefferson Street and along the Mississippi, she took the next morning's train to Beloit. She brought one large and one small suitcase, plus one canvas bag filled with edibles. She knew one Beloit address: Elvin's. It had been Albert Drinkwater's, too.

She was the last one off the train when it pulled into the Beloit Station. She laughed a little, only to herself she believed, as she made her way down the empty aisle. Was she getting cold feet? Then she did laugh out loud, remembering when she'd first heard the expression "cold feet" as a little girl, and thinking it had to do with ice.

It was April 12, 1915. She'd stopped wearing black three months earlier. Although she hadn't received a card from her brother since she'd returned to regular colors, she was confident he would be happy to see her here. She had sent the second telegram of her life—the first had told Elvin of their father's passing—to let him know she was arriving on this date, this train.

Elvin had not returned to Yarmouth for the funeral. And Albert Drinkwater, was he still in Beloit?

Finally she exited the carriage and took her first Wisconsin steps. She saw her suitcases on the cart next to the newsstand. She saw an unfamiliar newspaper with a familiar topic: *US Troops Reach France*. She looked left, right, and left again, but did not see Elvin. She was about to pull the larger of her two bags toward her when she felt a hand on her right arm. She looked into the deep eyes of Albert Drinkwater.

She turned toward him and without a thought, without an ounce of caution, she was kissing a man for the first time in her life. And again.

From the train station Albert walked her to a rooming house on Pleasant Street. She spent the first night in the room of old Mrs. Melcher, the owner. The next night, after a visit to the Justice of the Peace on Grand Avenue, Mr. and Mrs. Drinkwater closed their second-floor door to the outside world. Except for brief trips to the toilet room down the hall, they remained inside for three days.

Hazel had entered into so many new worlds. Albert, of course, and his body, but there was her body, too. She felt as if she were returning to the familiar, to something she'd once known but lost or misplaced. There was Albert's room, barely large enough for the small bed, a wooden chair, a shelf that doubled as a table, and a tiny wardrobe for his meager handful of clothing. And more, deeper than all of this, was the silence.

Albert had been so quiet in Yarmouth that Hazel had suspected, but had not confirmed, that he actually could not speak. She found it to be so. From his ever-present small notebook he handed her notes, explaining that he'd lost the power at age six, that he could hear poorly but adequately if he were spoken to clearly, slowly, and directly. She accepted it as another new but ordinary fact.

When he took pen and ink to her thigh and scripted his name in blue, however, she clutched his hands and wanted to hold them forever. And each year after, she never failed to rejoice at the first fall of snow.

After the End of School

This teacher thinks he's being clever but he doesn't know the half of it. *"It's not just the child whose life has dissolved; remember, the adults are crumbling, too."* Their daddy was barely out of the driveway when Millie and Lynn stopped sleeping and little Max shut down like a toy with an old battery, forming words only when absolutely necessary—"cereal's gone." Gone too, their daddy, my husband. Only ten feet in front of me, the child psychology instructor faded to a place I couldn't follow. I was working too hard to keep from sobbing.

Dissolving was an apt word. In a matter of months I'd dissolved from a confident, loving *and* loved university professor's wife to a night student at Scottsdale Community College. It wasn't my first experience of the campus, situated on the Salt River Indian Reservation, just fifteen minutes from our home, but the other visits had always involved cultural or political events, and they had always included Joe. As close as it was in miles, Scottsdale Community College, and summer school at that, was a world away from Arizona State University, but A.S.U. wasn't mine anymore.

Then this Dylan-like kid plops his hand on my desk. They're all Dylan now, some combination of cherubic or bearded, improbably long hair, army surplus jacket. The classroom was overwhelmingly female, but of the six or seven men, most looked just like him. The sixties were over, for heaven's sake, it was already 1972, but the fashions hadn't changed, not for the guys.

He was sitting in front of me, not even looking back, but somehow he'd shifted and stretched and there was his arm on my desk. His arm, his hand, my fingers, my tears.

I've committed a goodly number of wild acts in my life. The literature department at Smith College, coupled with dismal New England winters and the infusion of male energy from UMASS and Williams and Amherst, was more daring and treacherous than any outsider presumed, even in the early 50's. Especially in the early 50's. But here. Now. July, 1972. Clutching this boy's hand. This may top everything.

Nine o'clock arrived and the room emptied. We sat on a few moments before I released his hand and we walked into the desert air. Outside, he asked: "Do you want to sit awhile and talk?"

We walked to my station wagon, the rear littered as always with the remains of my children's day. Silence, then he began: "So, I've been part-time at the A.S.U. child care center and now I want to get my credential." He paused, but I wasn't ready for my turn, so he kept going. "It's crazy. I'm changing diapers–me, the baby boy of the family."

"How did you get started there?" It was a relief to think of a question.

"I was taking an Intro to Feminism course Senior Year and the class required volunteer hours. Pretty soon it turned kind of magical, surrounded by these little creatures and I got hired right after I graduated. I'm liking it a lot, not that I'd want to do it twenty-four hours."

Maybe I started to cry just a bit because he stopped talking and took my hands in his. Then he asked if I had kids–not that it wasn't obvious from the car–"I bet with kids you already know everything they're teaching us."

I took a breath, kept my hands where they were, and spoke real words: "I'm taking the class because I need a job. I need a job because my husband, Joe, has moved out. He rented a home in the Superstition Mountains with a law student. Blonde. Twenty-four."

It may have been the first time I'd strung those sentences together out loud.

"And, yes, I have three children: eleven, ten, and eight."

We sat and talked, and sometimes we sat and I cried, for almost an hour. He remembered that I was Ramona but I had to ask his name. It was Leo.

At one point, more like Cary Grant than flower child, he interrupted one of my crying interludes by proffering a clean, folded, white handkerchief. It was so sweet I started to cry even more.

I remembered the sitter and told him I had to go "right now." I kissed him on the cheek and said, as I had so many times, "thank you."

We had one class remaining, in two nights, for the final exam.

"I'll see you Thursday night?" I half-asked, half-demanded.

"Guaranteed," he said.

As he was opening the passenger door I watched myself slide over and lightly kiss him on the lips. "Thursday," I repeated to the man-child as he exited. I said it a few more times as I drove home.

I was almost late for the final class. I couldn't decide what to wear, which alternately appalled and amused me. But I was frantic, too. Joe had picked the kids up on schedule, bless his heartless heart, and was going to keep them for the night, so there were no witnesses to my performance. Just as I had clicked shut the front door, already sure to be late, I unlocked it and stepped inside for a scarf I'd purchased a year ago in Santa Fe, but never worn since. For some reason I wrapped it around my waist, and away I went, speeding east on Chaparral.

Oh, god, he'd spread his jacket over my desk. Do they go to school for that, or is it in their genes? In my head, I saw the word as *jeans*. Calm down, Ramona, you are no longer a sophomore!

After the test, which wasn't a tenth as difficult as dealing with three living children on a weekday morning, we took his van to a dark coffee shop I'd never noticed, called *Carpe Diem*. The van might have been an extra for *Easy Rider*. They talk all day about doing their own thing, but everything they do, everybody else on their block does, too. It's an army of self-proclaimed different drummers, wearing one uniform, following one drum. I recognized many of the tapes he had— one good thing about Joe having his students over to the house so often, you kept up to date on the music scene. I noticed the platform bed, too.

In the rush of leaving Tuesday night I had forgotten to return the handkerchief, so I had made sure to bring it, laundered, and folded again. He laughed, said that I could keep it, in fact he'd like for me to keep it. "I've got loads," he told me. "My grandma sends me some every birthday." I said I doubted he'd had so many birthdays that he could cavalierly give them away whenever he met a damsel in distress, but he laughed again and told me he had "another one coming in two weeks." That's when I found out how young he was.

I ventured a guess. "Will you be twenty-five?"

"Eventually," was the reply.

I was sitting in a hippie-van, someone's hand resting on the inside of my knee like it belonged there, and the someone said:

"My birthday is August 11th which makes me a 'double-Leo.' And," and here he hesitated, out of pride or embarrassment I couldn't tell, "I'll be twenty-two."

He started back in on the handkerchief story, that his dad had told him to "always carry a handkerchief, and matches, for the ladies," but I was busy doing the math. On the day of my wedding, on that Sunday in Chicago, that hand that felt so good right now had belonged to a toddler.

Odds were awfully good I was as old as his mother.

His Kris Kristofferson cassette was playing as he drove us back from the café to my car, something about "help get me through the night."

I can't believe I've lived in this desert so long. When I think of those autumns in Northampton, the Smith campus swirling in colors I'd never seen before, nor seen since, I am again stunned at the turns my life has taken. I was home for Christmas my senior year, had come back to Chicago on the Twentieth Century as I always did, and that's when I met Joe. He'd been there five years, handling baggage at LaSalle Street Station to put himself through the U. of Chicago. At that point he was just a few months shy of his doctorate in British Drama. He was dizzying and we married a week after my graduation. We moved around, Corvallis, then Missoula, but when we came here, tenure track, we bought the house. And when the tenure letter arrived we burned my diaphragm right in the fireplace. Joe used his deepest professorial voice: "And thus, we discern the writer's intent. Always remember, students, if there is a fireplace in the first scene, in a drama set in Scottsdale, Arizona, it *will* be used."

Millie was born ten months to the day and Lynn fourteen months after that. Max followed Lynn by two full years.

A week after the Child Psych. class ended, Leo called the house. Millie answered, hollered for me, and said as she gave me the receiver: "it's some boy."

We had a few more phone conversations, then after another week, on another night when the kids would be with Joe, we met back at the coffee shop. We were there ten minutes before I was driving home, his van following me. That night someone shared my bed and my body for the first time in a year.

I only had to wait three days for the next time. Then two days, then two days again, then, for the next month, we were together almost every night.

Leo said he hadn't taken any classes from Joe but I believe my Leo, who had been an English major, was capable of a white lie. It would have been in one of the university's large auditoriums, to be sure, so it's safe to say they'd never spoken one-to-one, but the way Leo described some lectures he had attended, I had to wonder. I didn't know what to think about that. I also didn't know how not to think about it.

Leo took me to a club in Phoenix for my birthday to see, as he put it, "the coolest singer ever." He told me he had her albums, but he'd never seen her in person, and he was counting the days and hours, then blocks as we drove up. I hadn't heard her songs but I knew who Dory Previn was. I didn't know how much Leo knew. I often didn't know. Dory and Andre Previn had been married for years, a model public couple, he the composer and conductor, she the songwriter. A model couple until he dumped her for a hot Hollywood starlet, Mia Farrow, blonde and beautiful, as starlets tend to be, as the triggers for divorce tend to be. With Leo beside me, I could handle her angry lyrics; alone, I would have fled into the night, haunted by her clever story-songs about young women and betrayal.

If I hadn't sworn to never again cry in front of Leo, this would have been the night, would have been the song.

That night I had to give him the lecture. "Leo, this is all good fun, but please, it isn't 'love.' It's good, let's just enjoy it."

"But you say it sometimes."

"I know, I know, and I apologize. It's not fair. Let's just seize the day."

The kids were so sweet about the whole thing. Leo always carried licorice and he was good at sharing, so he was halfway home just with that. They climbed on him as if he were a puppy whenever they got the chance, in the house, in the yard, and on the river when we went up to Fort McDowell. Maybe he was the new toy they needed, the special thing you take on a train to get you to the next place.

One Sunday in October I kept him longer than usual. Normally if he stayed over on a Saturday night, he was gone before ten, for "Sunday softball"—with his buddies—it turns out hippies still played softball—but this time I found ways to keep him occupied. Joe was bringing the kids back at one and I wanted to show him what I had. It was childish, and it wasn't even news, because I'd told Joe the week before, and the kids surely had said something much earlier than that, but I'd seen his Lindsey too often to not want to do a little bragging of my own. Childish, but real. We were sitting in the patio when I panicked: what if Joe brings her? He never had brought her to the house, but what if he did? I didn't want Leo to see her. I worried enough—I hated myself for it—about the young women he saw every day, at his work, in his apartment complex, on the streets, they were everywhere, *sans* bra, *sans* who knew what else. Still, they didn't need to show up here. I almost called Joe, almost sent Leo off, just dithered, twisting the ends of my hair like I was fourteen.

I wonder if there's a word for the handshake between a husband and a boyfriend, and would it be still another word if we changed the terms from husband to *ex-husband,* or boyfriend to *lover.* Words! Lover. *Current* lover. *Boy* friend. My mouth parched when Joe materialized as if he owned the place (which is still something to be resolved), his dark body contrasting handsomely, as he knew only too well, against his bright tennis whites. Objectively, he remained a good-looking man.

Subjectively, which is where I lived most of the time, I wished he'd move to Alaska, or Zanzibar, or anywhere in between, as long as it was far from here. Except not really, because of the kids.

Joe came alone and there he was, towering over Leo, my slender lion. Leo stood as tall as he could, barely an inch taller than me, with his sun-reddened moustache, his hair six inches longer than mine, his innocent eyes. He looked as if he were in the principal's office. Perhaps he was thinking he'd been caught completely inside the cookie jar. My smile must have developed into a laugh.

"What's funny?" one or both inquired.

"Nothing. It just came out, I guess." But it was my epiphany: whatever else you could say about me, and I could say worse than anyone, I chose fine-looking men.

"Okay. I'll see you Wednesday. Good to meet you, Ki–, uh, Leo." And Joe was gone almost as soon as he had arrived.

I pressed against Leo but avoided his face. Joe had almost called him "Kid."

Leo had driven to Southern California for his mother's birthday, which was just a week after mine, and Joe had the kids, so I had a weekend to myself. It would be the mom's 49th, making her six years older than me. I considered whether Webster's Dictionary would see this fact as a sufficient example of "consolation," but I didn't look.

When Joe and I married, it was different. Richard Nixon was barely the vice-president, much less a twice-elected president. We didn't even have television in those days, though a few friends did. We just loved each other. I was to read some time later that "love is eternal for as long as it lasts."

I never saw it coming. It being Lindsey. Maybe he didn't either. At least…ah, there's another ridiculous expression: "at least." But, for lack of a better term, at least he told me himself, directly. Immediately.

Leo and I were sprawled in bed, the sheets drenched, the swamp cooler again no match for our own midnight heat. This was a year when even November temperatures hit the nineties.

"I'm just so fucking happy," he said. With that, he kissed me, an angel kiss on my shoulder. He was starting to say "fucking" and "fuck" a lot. I was of two minds: I neither liked nor used the word, nor had Joe, at least not in my presence, but the last thing I wanted was for my lion to wake up and truly realize he was sleeping with the class of 1952.

We took the kids to Fort McDowell a few times. I wasn't sure, the first time, because for so long, picnics there had been a *family* thing, and only recently the kids and I had ventured to go without Joe. But, again, they were fine.

The river was running low, which was always my favorite, and all five of us waded and splashed each other. When we ate, Leo couldn't stop talking about the potato salad, and even more, my deviled eggs. "These are like my mom's," he said. And said again. Even Millie and Lynn were laughing before Leo realized that he was sounding a little kid-like.

We were naked in my bathroom, our reflections staring back at us. The kids were away and for two days we didn't wear a stitch of clothing. I loved that leonine body, golden and smooth and hard. That was the moment I knew it was temporary. I had always known, but in front of the mirror clarity rang the bell and stayed for tea. I was a swimmer and blessed with healthy genes, and for a woman of a certain age, I couldn't complain. But standing beside a boy almost a presidential term from twenty-five. I moaned.

"Look at my body."

"What do you think I'm doing?" From behind me he wrapped his arms around me, his hands across my chest.

"No, Leo, I'm serious. Look at the lines, the wear and tear. It is not a young body. It will never again be one."

"Turn around, lady, *carpe* the fucking *diem*."

Lately it was more like once or twice a week. Leo had more hours at work, plus he was working part-time at a restaurant, and he had also joined a second softball league, this one co-ed. He also had moved into "not really a collective," but a big house, with three other guys. It was a while later when he added, "oh, yeah, there's two girls, too."

At first we didn't give each other gifts, another of my rules, but he pestered me until we reached an accommodation. "But," I said, "they cannot cost more than two dollars." We had some fun with it, I admit, silly little things passing between us.

He was, in his words, "super-excited," because over Christmas he was going down to Mexico, to Rocky Point, also called Puerto Penasco, to spend a week on the beach. He'd be one of three drivers, going with most of his household, plus a batch of co-workers. By this time I, too, was working, at a Montessori-like school, but at my stage in life you didn't run off to Mexico for the holidays. Not that he'd invited me. In a Salvation Army store in Phoenix I found a used copy of *One Hundred Years of Solitude*. I hadn't yet read it but it looked to be an appropriate novel for the "mythical"–again, his word–trip.

I gave him the book and on the inside I'd written: *To my Lion. I paid exactly twenty-five cents for this. Please do let me read it after you, and thank you for shining your light into my solitude. Love, Ramona.*

Yes, I'd always known. And, yes, I've always known the difference between *knowing* and *understanding*. And a week after New Year's, at an hour when I normally would have been at work, I watched from my bedroom as my cowardly lion scurried through the late-morning shadows, along the driveway and around to the back. On the wrought-iron table, the one Joe, Leo and I had once so awkwardly surrounded, Leo set down a package, and then raced back to his van where a young woman waited. She was not blonde but she might as well have been.

At home that day with a sudden flu, sitting in a lump against two pillows, unable to sleep, barely able to read, the sheets miserable with crumpled tissues and the morning's Arizona Republic, I watched it all.

The van disappeared–that is the correct word–and after another hour I found the strength to leave the bed. I staggered into the sunshine to find a bookstore-new hardcover copy of *One Hundred Years of Solitude*, the last gift of my lion. Scribbled on the title page was "thank you." I sat at the table and began to read.

A Gentle Rage

I've lived in this house 45 years. I'm 91. You do the math.

Yesterday I went to see the house and neighborhood of my youth—not my thirties, but my childhood. That was a long time ago. Yesterday is already pretty far back, too.

I almost wrote "yesterday I drove to see the house" but that, unfortunately, would be a lie. I haven't driven anywhere in six months, since the day my kids descended like interveners from that television show, and presto, they had my keys.

Oh, they praised me to the skies, my courage, the rightness of my decision, how wonderful it was I had made the choice, not them, but God it happened fast. That's the new deal—and I do recall the real New Deal—things creep along, just creep and creep, but in a flash, everything changes. As my tax guy said, when I told him I intended to drop dead in my home: "We all do, but you, my friend, are one fall away from something very different."

So now, in addition to the unmitigated joy of moving with a walker with two tennis balls, there's more. If I want to go anywhere, someone has to take me. I've been driving for 75 years. Try stopping that on a dime. It's not easy. What it is, is the shits, pardon the expression. And, no, I won't digress into the real shits, and that delight. I won't. I keep saying: "Never get old," and everybody laughs, thinking I'm being funny.

But I want to tell you about that trip. We left at nine and arrived by eleven. Obviously it wasn't terribly far but I hadn't been back in, in, in a long time. I don't like the expression "in decades" but I could use it often if I wanted. I don't.

Like they say, everything looked smaller. So what. I'm smaller, too. I used to be five-nine, but now I'm barely five-five, and my pants keep sliding off. My license says five-nine, for all the good that does me.

We got there, my son driving his silent Prius, me in the suicide seat, and he parked in front of the house. "This is it, right, Dad?" He had a Google print-out and a GPS thing. I said yes. Maybe it was.

Doesn't make any difference, you just do what they say, and say what they want. It's easier.

I'm sure I slept all the way home, and probably most of the way up there. I know I missed the bridge in both directions. I remember crossing the bay for years, from a different house, when I worked in the city. I remember driving my car onto the morning ferry, coffee on the way over and two beers coming home. I always stood outside, in sun or mist or fog or rain, it didn't matter. I was alive.

It's all past tense now.

Honest as a Sister Can Be

"We lived under this same roof but your mom was raised by wolves. We always knew that door from opposite sides." Aunt Rosie performed a dual role regarding my mom, as both chief celebrant and royal accuser. Thanksgivings came more frequently every year, so it seemed, and it was with particular relish that she served the prom night story. It was a tradition she made new each November, her eyes flashing, her voice rising and falling along a musical scale only she knew. Even her hands and arms played their parts, their instincts honed by well-orchestrated stage directions.

Aunt Rosie, Dr. Rosaline DeNatale in her professional life, was just fourteen months older than Mama and one class ahead in school. As kids they were jerked up and down the valley, following my grandfather's endless and fruitless climb-up-the-ladder-of-success schemes until they settled in this very house on Mama's fifteenth birthday, May 6, 1963, which coincided with the 32nd birthday of Willie Mays. Mama loved baseball, batted and threw left-handed, played it in schoolyards and streets in all those thirsty towns: pick-up games, work-ups, five-hundred and fly-up, so sharing her birthday with the Say Hey Kid was icing on the cake. In fact, when she took up knitting, in a forced term of inactivity that fortuitously eased my arrival in 1964, she emblazoned a blue baby blanket with the Tallulah Bankhead line:

There have been only two geniuses in the world:
Willie Mays and Willie Shakespeare.

One can do worse than to be tucked in nightly with Will, Willie and Tallulah. Adding to that, my own birthday is April 23rd, making Shakespeare exactly 400 years older than me. So I have some catching up to do. And yes, that is why I am a Juliet, and I've been forever grateful that I'm neither Ophelia nor Cordelia. Or Tallulah.

My mother came and went. She was the distant older cousin who dropped in without warning, hugged me and praised me and stared at me, and just as quickly disappeared again, often as I slept. I saw her once or twice a year, no more, but she always sent something in April. Or May. When I turned eight it was a needlepoint splayed with red roses and what turned out to be a mangled version of a Grateful Dead lyric: *Honest as Denver.* My grandmother tacked it over my bed, cooed over the lettering, kissed my cheek and told me for the millionth time "your mother loves you." She added: "She is so artistic." And: "Maybe she's in Denver."

But Denver, if that's where she had been, was a long time ago, and I was almost two decades beyond that 8th birthday. Aunt Rosie had paused in her telling, respecting the ceremonial slicing of the gingerbread and the pumpkin pie, but once the whipped cream had made the rounds, she returned to her theme.

"Your mother claimed to be above such bourgeois trifles as the Junior Prom. It was my very first formal dance, and I was going with my chemistry lab partner's boyfriend's cousin's best friend, if you can follow that. It wasn't anything I did, or he did, for that matter, because Eleanor and her boyfriend arranged it all. And Ronnie, my shining prince, I hoped, was already a freshman in college. We'd only actually met once in the flesh and never gone on a date, but when he called I jumped out of my socks, and when I found out *why* he was calling, you'll excuse me for saying I almost peed in my pedal-pushers. Remember, we were new in town.

"It was the end of May, supposedly the hottest May in Stockton's infernal history. We didn't have air conditioning and the fans we did have were flat-out pooped, the poor things. We were supposed to meet Eleanor and her boyfriend for dinner at Valentino's, on the river, and then go on to the dance. Valentino's must have closed twenty years ago. The prom was at a hotel downtown that's long gone, too." Here she paused, gazing across the years, blinking in wonderment at the passage of time. Here, always, she caught herself, took a breath, and continued.

"I was upstairs with Grandma ripping out most of my hair trying to keep it in place. It was suffocating and I was sweating like a barnyard animal. I'd like to tell you I was glowing, but I was pouring the real stuff. Then I heard it. I heard a rumble, like sound effects from a Saturday afternoon movie, and I looked out the dormer window and saw it, his black Corvette. A 1962 Chevrolet Corvette. I'd been told about that car but this was the first time I'd seen it with my own eyes.

"My heart still thumps when I see one of those beauties. Mother – your grandmother–went down first, mostly to make sure Grandpa didn't scare him away, and also to stall for me so I could get my breath back. I know Grandpa was always a pussycat for you, but he had a bark in his day. I was the bride in the tower who's not supposed to see the groom before the wedding, but I refused to back away from that window. He sauntered up the walk like he was in a magazine, tall and broad-shouldered with his mess of black hair slicked just so, scrubbed and proud in his baby blue tuxedo, and the car behind him was right off one of those billboards. I was going to ride in that car! I perched upstairs on my little chair and inhaled like a yogi. I wasn't sure where your mother was, I thought maybe she'd gone to the park, but it turned out she was sitting on the porch steps as Ronnie arrived. And you know she was the dark one even then, always with the golden tan, while I was stuck with long sleeve shirts and floppy hats if I ever dared venture into the sun. She was wearing the shortest *and* tightest cut-offs imaginable, and one of Daddy's raggedy old shirts, missing a button or two on top, and tied in a knot above her navel. No shoes. No make-up. And, no doubt, no brassiere. If anyone could glow in 94 degree heat, she was the one.

"Ronnie took forever to get past her. I was dying. I died and died and died. My tinny alarm clock kept ticking and I kept dying. Daddy paced the hardwood floor: living room to kitchen, kitchen to living room. At the foot of the stairs my mother steamed and glared at the door, praying, as I was, for the deliverance of the doorbell. Five minutes, maybe more, I don't know. Did you ever see those photos of Sue Lyon, the girl who played Lolita in that movie? No, that was way before your time, but when I think about your mother that day, that's what I think about. Or Raquel Welch in anything.

"Thankfully, my mother yanked the door open and hauled him in. I can only imagine the look she gave *your* mother before she slammed the door shut between them. The echo exploded up the stairs and I couldn't wait another second. I rushed down as gracefully as I could in my ridiculous high heels, hanging onto the rail with both hands. Years later, when I first heard someone say 'looking like a deer caught in the headlights,' I knew exactly what they meant. Even in the photograph Daddy took, Ronnie's an alien on the wrong planet. Without a map. With a broken space ship. He was transfixed by whatever he'd experienced on the porch. He was sweating so much I probably looked cool as a cucumber next to him, and I promise you, I was anything but that. He shifted from foot to foot, kept his eyes to the floor, couldn't talk to me, wouldn't even look at me. I'm sure he didn't *want* to look at me, in my silly frou-frou prom dress that I'd slaved over for ten sweltering nights. After your mother arching her back and God knows what else outside, I'm sure he thought there was nothing worth spit on this side of the door. And that's where we were, right in this room. Your mother could throw like a boy but her body was all-girl. Woman.

"He squeezed his wilting bouquet like a life-rope, but he released it, and I traded him a corsage. He was so pale my mother ordered him to sit while she ran for the pitcher of water. He barely exhaled, still wasn't speaking, didn't even say 'thank you,' just gulped a twelve ounce glass of weak lemon water. I desperately wanted to leave except I knew he'd start drooling when he saw her again. Still, the front porch was the only way to his car, and the car was the only way to the prom, so what was I to do? Daddy reminded him to drive carefully, and that prompted him to reach into his pocket for his keys, I guess to assure everyone, without a word, since he was incapable of that, that he knew what he was doing, that he was reliable, but he came up empty. He gaped at his open right hand as if it were a traitor. He tried all his pockets. Nothing but a thin wallet. He started looking around as if he could spot the keys on the newspaper-strewn table by my father's chair, or on the mantel of the fireplace that mocked us each torrid day.

Nothing. 'Must be in the car,' he muttered, his first sound, and out we rushed.

"To an empty porch, for which I passionately praised God, until Ronnie screamed: 'She took my 'Vette!'"

California cops, and I am one, refer to car theft as a "ten-eight-five-one." All the judges, the lawyers, and the perps call it the same thing. For Mama, her 10851 was the beginning of a lifelong relationship with the criminal codes of California, Arizona, and Nevada. For Aunt Rosie, it was the first of 10,000 nights with Ronald DeNatale.

Pancakes

After they ordered, Jake spotted a discarded newspaper in the next booth and snagged it. He was the one who, had it been possible, would have arranged for a paper to be delivered daily to the door of his dented but beloved bus as they rolled across the nation. It was 1970, for Christ's sake. Couldn't somebody figure out how to do that? He probably would have sold his new boots to pay for the subscription.

"I'll read the heavy stuff," he said, "and soften it for you. You know, sometimes you're like a baby who can't handle hard food."

"Well, fuck you, too," Robby snapped. "All I ever said, *once*, was I don't need to hear the body count every fucking day."

"I'm just saying, some people major in history, others read novels. An observation, not a criticism."

He was bringing up this crap again? Just because he didn't relish the negative, did that make him a Pollyanna? It pissed him off, and it was the only thing between them that did. He tried again.

"Yes, the world is fucked up. I get it. Nixon and napalm and nuts with knives, yes, I know. But I choose to look at the other stuff, too. Is that so bad?"

Jake's face was pink, indicating he knew he'd crossed the 'do-not-cross' line.

"I'm sorry, man, I am. I'm afflicted with a touch of the old flippancy today, I know." And he added: "I know that it hurts others worse than it hurts me."

He extended his arm, resting his hand on top of the napkin dispenser.

"Shake?" They did.

The breakfasts arrived, toast was buttered, syrup was poured, and happy chewing took the stage until a new subject was raised.

"Unrelated to any of this, Rob, I got to tell you something I heard yesterday in the drugstore in, where was it? Fort Madison, I think, right after we got crossed up into Iowa. You were still in that record store. I told the clerk I liked their little downtown but it was too bad that so many of the storefronts were empty. And she said 'this place has gone downhill since all the Negroes started to move here from Chicago and St. Louis.' And she had all these nice religious posters on the wall behind her."

"God bless America," he managed to say.

"Lordy, yes. It made me want to take a shower. But I am gonna look at the paper now, if that's all right."

"Knock yourself out. Let me know if the war's over."

He returned to his serious stack of buckwheat pancakes and its side of bacon and eggs. The bacon alone could have fed a small troop of Boy Scouts. They hadn't had a breakfast like this in a long time.

"Shit! Shit, shit, shit."

"Can's over that way, I think, just past the cigarettes."

"Not funny, asshole, listen to this." And Jake read aloud, carefully enunciating each syllable of what he now already knew:

Guitarist Jimi Hendrix has died after collapsing at a party in London. Police say there was no question of foul play. A number of sleeping pills were found at the house in Notting Hill Gate and they have been taken away for analysis.

"Oh, man, I'm sorry," he said. "Jesus Christ, what the Hell, man?"

Jake stood, folded the paper against the ketchup and steak sauce bottles, and walked toward the door. "I'll be back, just some air."

He watched him go out into the September sunshine. The autumn equinox, or solstice, whichever it was, was coming soon, but the days were still feeling more summer than not. The good weather abruptly felt wrong. This shouldn't be happening at all, and if did, it shouldn't be learned about on a shiny morning. Stupid. He picked up the paper:

Hendrix, 27, was born in Seattle, Washington, but rose to fame in Britain with his band the Jimi Hendrix Experience. He will be remembered as a key figure in the music world who transformed electric guitar-playing using distortion, feedback and sheer volume to create a revolutionary new sound.

He knew all that, but for the first time, he thought twenty-seven to be really young. He started to ask himself who he might be by that age but chased the question away. He pictured his Hendrix albums back home in L.A., the cassettes in the van, and his buddy outside: His buddy, the one who played softball really well and guitar even better.

He ate slowly, trying to savor each bite, and forgetting almost every time. The waitress re-filled his ice water and checked if everything was okay. She wore the classic restaurant-server outfit and looked a bit like an all-knowing mother on a sit-com, but they did not talk about what was in the paper. He could tell that she had been about to ask what happened to his friend but had decided not to, and he admired the decision.

He read a little more but found nothing worth knowing. Unless he had overlooked it, there was no new draft policy, and without doubt, the war was thriving. Newspapers were mixed blessings, at best.

When he had eaten more than was wise—but what else was there to do—he asked for Jake's to be boxed up. He paid and tipped, and walked outside. They had parked near a colorful tree that was still leafy, although there also were leaves on the pavement that made a crunchy sound as he walked through them. He found him under the tree, sitting against the trunk, strumming quietly on his guitar.

He put the box of lukewarm bacon, scrambled eggs and toast on the floor of the passenger seat and sat on a bench about ten yards from the tree. He listened for an hour to familiar tunes as well as re-imagined or invented ones. After an extended exploration of "While My Guitar Gently Weeps," the music stopped. Jake looked up for the first time, a sad smile on his face, and pulled himself up from his spot. As they walked to the van they heard quiet clapping and turned to see a mom and dad and a couple of kids sitting at an outside table on the grass. The man flashed the peace sign and they reciprocated.

The guitar was put back into its case, returned to the van and tucked safely among the pillows and sleeping bags. He drove, and the guitarist ate cold eggs with a plastic fork.

A Good Day to be Born

Arthur was born in the late afternoon as the radio blared and the fathers paced, paced and listened, one ear to the ballgame, the other to the screams escaping the door to New York Public's maternity ward. Arthur's father always claimed the nurse came to get him exactly as Mel Allen called the Joe DiMaggio blast that won game two of the 1950 World Series. Arthur's grandfather, on the other hand, swore he got the call from his son-in-law two hours after the birth, and that it was *the phone call* that coincided with DiMaggio's shot. Both agreed on the inning, tenth, and the pitcher, Robin Roberts.

The new father went along with his wife's wish to name their son Arthur, after her brother who had died in the Philippines just as the war was ending. He went along but he still dreamed of "Joe DiMaggio Silverman" on a birth certificate, on a diploma, on a professional baseball contract. He did understand that even the big home run couldn't trump his wife's memory of her brother, a brother he had never met.

While DiMaggio circled the Shibe Park bases in Philadelphia that October day, another war was thriving, this time in Korea, and Arthur's father was the right age. Even with the baby's birth it was clear he would be called soon. By January of '52 he was in uniform in Texas. Four months later he was cooking in Korea–he had been a cook in the Bronx–and that is where he met DiMaggio. The Yankee Clipper was touring different bases now, rallying the troops in the truest sense of the expression, and Arthur's father was in his mess hall when, without warning, DiMaggio and six Hollywood starlets dropped in for lunch.

DiMaggio was shorter, up close, than he'd appeared in Yankee Stadium's spacious center field. In the batter's box, even seen from the distant bleachers, he'd stood tall, his god-like body poised to turn on a pitch. He was smoking, too, and exhausted, but took a moment with each G.I. Arthur's father wished more deeply than ever his son was another Joe DiMaggio.

He approached him after the meal and told the story of his son's birth. He told it his way, not his father-in-law's way. The Clipper smiled, wished nothing but good luck for his son, hoped that "maybe he'd be a Yankee one day." Then he was gone with the starlets, motoring under heavy escort to another base, another show. This camp had not had the luck of a drawing a show, but to Arthur's father, they'd drawn the high card.

When Arthur turned nineteen, the war was in Vietnam. He was three thousand miles from home, one of a micro-culture of New Yorkers populating UCLA's Rieber Hall dormitory.

On December 1st of 1969 the nation crowded into family rooms to watch the lottery. For the first time since World War II, and for the very first time on television, young men were receiving individual numbers from the Selective Service System.

At home his mother and father sat, not in their usual spots—she on the couch and he in his recliner—but together on the couch, the quilt made by her mother across their knees. They held hands. On the wall above the television were black and white photographs of her brother, one in his military uniform, and one at age fourteen, guiding her as she learned to ride a bicycle. There were photos of other family members, too, but many of those were in color, and most were alive. The newest picture, not six months old, was their son in cap and gown, holding his high school diploma.

"Should we call him?" For the first time she wondered if naming him after her brother had been a good idea.

"No, not now, not yet," his father decided. He had been thinking about Korea and also about the story in the paper about a local kid who'd overdosed on some drug. And then there was the family around the corner whose kid had been killed last month in Vietnam. That kid, Dominic Something, had been three years ahead of Arthur in school.

"I'm so afraid," she whispered. "When that man brought the telegram Mrs. Bianchi looked like she'd been hit with a brick. Honey, he's just a baby. They're all babies."

Arthur's father squeezed her hand and made her look right at him.

"It's going to be okay. He was born on a good day."

On the television it was about to begin. Parents and sons across the nation edged a bit closer to their screens. Distances collapsed. Arthur's father noticed how warm it was in the room and how the hall light climbed the stairway. The first number was drawn.

Standing Room Only

It was on December 1st that Arthur and 100% of his floor-mates, sixty college freshmen, plus the R.A., the upper-classman who had his own room, and in return the responsibility for holding their hands when needed, packed the television room to watch the lottery. The lottery. Five years ago, at fourteen, he'd read Shirley Jackson's chilling short story, "The Lottery." As he maneuvered into a niche near the back, he massaged his head to rid it of Jackson's tale. By wordless consent the young men pushed the furniture to the walls and stood for the entire show. "The show" was an odd term for what they were about to see, yet that's what had been on flyers in the dining hall and the elevators: *"The show! Be There: Get Lucky or Kiss Your Ass Goodbye."*

Fall quarter roared toward finals and he had barely kissed a girl, much less "get lucky" in the way everyone else was doing. Every weekend another friend boldly or shyly bragged about sex, real sex, and all he did was read about it. He wasn't sure he could stand four years of this if fiction was the closest he'd ever get.

The boys who would be men were scared. They hadn't done this before. Nobody had done this before, not since the dinosaur days of 1942. In minutes somebody was going to pluck little cylinders out of a drum. Inside were all the possible birth dates to be matched to a list of the numbers from 1 to 366 on the wall. No, they didn't forget Leap Year. The date that matched with number one, every nineteen year old boy in the country with that birthday would be first in line to be drafted. The dream date would be number three hundred and sixty-six; those guys wouldn't see a drill sergeant until the Red Army marched from San Francisco to and across the Mississippi River. The story was if your number was in the first third, you were cooked. If you were in the last third, you were golden. If you drew an in-between number, roughly one-twenty to two-forty, you hadn't learned a thing. You were still stuck in the middle with little clue how to plan your life. That was the whole idea, they said, that by giving young men this information, they could in fact plan their lives without the uncertainty of the current stunningly random draft system.

It was true that as long as they were in college, taking and passing a full load of classes, they were safe. Safe until they graduated, or dropped out, or sneezed in the wrong place. No, that latter happenstance, the sneezing in the wrong place, was the sort of thing that was no longer a factor. As long as you or your parents could afford college, you were okay. Naturally, the sweeping changes had no effect on the wealthy. Even in the chaos of 1969, some things remained sacred. Nobody had any illusions that a rich kid couldn't avoid the whole deal, and nobody had a single illusion that ninety-nine percent of them wouldn't do exactly that.

Safe, then, until they graduated, or dropped out. Arthur had no clue what his own plans might be, even apart from the threat of Vietnam. School was okay but it was no passion. Was he where he belonged? Six high school friends were on their way to Vietnam. Another, two years older, had burned his draft card and was in prison. Still another was feigning homosexuality, but also applying to divinity school, covering all bets. Arthur didn't know anyone in Canada but he knew people who did.

The room was usually noisy, to watch football games. This was different. He thought he knew everyone at least on a some-name basis. One guy everybody called "Cowboy." Several others were last-name guys, like Grauman and Preston and Rippinger, and he couldn't have said their first names on a bet. In September he had nudged his own name to Art, but sometimes he didn't respond when someone used it. He would always be Arthur at home.

Street performers had hit campus earlier in the week: *Join the army, see the world: Kill a gook, screw a girl. Get the clap, a purple heart: Some penicillin, a brand new start.*

He didn't want any of that, not that way, and he certainly wasn't a killer, of "gooks" or anybody else. Was he lucky or unlucky? He couldn't say. Maybe his luck was waiting for something really important, like this lottery.

One of Cowboy's big hats perched on the television and each guy had dropped a dollar into it. The money was a consolation prize for the sucker whose birthday was drawn first. Arthur never wished ill on anyone but he implored the gods of fate to spare him that one.

He was nineteen. Somebody thought he was a man. Who was he to plan his life? Washington's good intentions, if that's what they were, were wasted on him.

This morning his US History professor told a story: Just before World War One, the Great War, "remember, the war to end all wars until the next one came along," the famous Washington D.C. cherry trees were planted, thanks to the Japanese Ambassador, who brought cuttings from the even more famous Tokyo cherry trees. The trees, thousands of them, were the gifts of the Japanese people. Then in World War Two, the United States bombed the hell out of Tokyo, wiping out the trees, and a large amount of people, too, so after the war, the U.S. sent cuttings of the Washington trees back to Tokyo. Nothing to replace the people.

The crowd crept even closer to the television to hear the first date. Arthur saw guys holding hands. He heard someone praying. He heard his own heartbeat.

"September Fourteen." Dave Rippinger–that was his name, Dave!–cursed and kicked the table, sending television, hat and cash flying to the floor, before storming out.

Fifty-nine remained.

Cookie and George

The first George was my sister's age, two years older than me. *His* sister, Missy, was in my class, and they lived down the street in a house that backed up to the creek that gave the town its name, so from day one I knew who he was. He was forever the tallest guy on the block. Everyone tried to get George to play basketball but he never went out for a team. He played at recess, and in P.E., but that's all. He'd rather draw pictures.

"It's a game, guys, it's just hearts or foursquare or Risk. Coach thinks it's war, and who needs that?" Even in Art Class, where he was really good, he never put his drawings into competitions.

He was always George. Never anything else. No, that's not true, because once I heard some jocks call him Georgie-the-queer. I looked away real quick, but I heard the coach laughing with them. Who knows? And even then, when I knew almost nothing, I knew enough not to worry about who liked what. Who cares? They were jerks, I knew that much.

The second George was George only to his teachers. To the rest of the universe, from his seventh birthday on, he was "Cookie," because that was the word that enticed him from a dead-perfect but rapidly airless old refrigerator during hide-and-seek on that very birthday: the word likely saved his life.

George is not an unusual name, but we only had the two, even in a high school of almost 500 students.

As life does on occasion imitate art, Cookie proved to be one sweet kid. He was adored by all: Little kids, dogs, big kids, teachers, parents, the whole town. Being nothing but himself, he charmed. His smile calmed you, his laugh made people grin without knowing why. He asked you questions because he wanted to know the answers. By the time he was seventeen, the girls, and doubtless a few moms, longed to share his company, and maybe one or two did. Boys liked to be with him, too, but not for the same reasons. I suppose dads would have, too, but we didn't see many fathers in our neighborhood, even counting those who actually lived there.

George and my sister graduated on schedule as Missy and Cookie and I finished our sophomore years. George's mother, who worked in the dry cleaning place two towns away, urged him to go to college, but he declined.

"Not now, anyway," he told her, and us. "I'd go if I had a reason, but right now I'd just be taking up desk space." He said: "As soon as we get Missy through, I'll probably go. You know me, if I want it, I'll do it." Instead, he hired on at the cannery, the town's biggest employer.

George hoisted bottles, cans, crates and pallets of tomato sauce, chili, and ketchup six days a week. My mom's boyfriend that year worked there, too, and told me "that George is skinny, but he's a mother of a worker." This boyfriend, Archie, looked pretty strong himself but it never came out at our place. The one thing he did lift was my mom's real diamond ring, from when she was married to my dad. Old Archie grabbed it one night and we never saw him again. It took awhile, but eventually my mom agreed it was a fair trade.

Nine months into his job, George got a letter from Uncle Sam. He was drafted. After a quick bout of basic training in a different part of the state he was off to Vietnam. My sister sometimes got letters but she never told me anything. How all of us could have been so clueless about the draft, I have no idea.

Two years after George's graduation, Missy and I were practicing our own "commencement walk" across the makeshift stage in the gym. We had three days of practice to learn how to climb three steps, walk to the center, accept a diploma, and exit the other side. I guess it was the only thing they could do to slow down the clock. Strange pedagogy.

On the program, Missy was co-valedictorian. I was not the other one, but I was one of the 112 names listed alphabetically. Cookie did not make it. He had liked Auto Shop, and Wood Shop, and nothing in between, and dropped out junior year. He was already eighteen so it was his choice. Fortunately, his mom's hamburger joint was *the* place in town, and without the nuisance of the school day, he served burgers and shakes from noon to eight, and still got to see everybody.

Every graduation week shocks. For three years, every day lasted forever as we trudged toward unimaginable futures. Now, entire weeks were flashing by like minimum days. Even the chunk of the senior class that hates school is struck dumb, thinking: "Well, dang, what am I supposed to do now?" Our class –"we are mighty, we are great, we are the class of '68"–so radical, so hip, was fooled just like all the others. One moment we were freshmen; the next, we were getting measured for caps and gowns. And, if you were eighteen and male, getting mail from the draft board.

Still, our year *was* different. I had cut my morning classes on April 4th to walk in the hills with Cookie but the car radio shouted that someone had murdered Martin Luther King. We still hiked but didn't talk much. In June, just after I'd gone to bed, my mom came in to say Bobby Kennedy had been shot, on live television. Graduation was three days away.

Campus was dead-silent the day after Kennedy. Missy and I were sitting on a bench, sheltered by our favorite oak tree, at last signing each other's yearbook, when Mr. Mayfield, the vice-principal, materialized as only he could, and told her to follow him.

"Hold my stuff, I'll be right back." Clutching my yearbook to her chest, she left with Mayfield, both walking quickly. I figured it was co-valedictorian stuff. I didn't see her for two hours. When I did, she still held my yearbook, but she also held the knowledge that her brother George had been dead for a week, "died a hero," Mayfield and the army guy repeated, as they could find nothing else to say. Missy and her mother, who had come to school in the army car, clutched each other on Mayfield's mock-leather couch, portraits of championship football teams grinning down at them.

It would be a month before we returned each other's yearbook, our messages hopelessly out-of-date. She skipped the ceremony, skipped her speech.

Despite Kennedy, despite George, graduation-week continued. Those last few nights we partied on the hill behind school, drinking and smoking until we were wasted. Some kissed, some groped, some with cars did more. Missy was home with her mom so I hung out with Cookie. Missy told me I should go out, so I did. Cookie never missed those nights that flitted between boisterous and bittersweet. He promised he would be at graduation, "in the front row!"

Only four hours until *Pomp and Circumstance,* Missy still in seclusion, I went to *George's.* You could say the hamburger stand was the town's third George, named by and for Cookie's dad, a guy most of us had never seen, who lived somewhere in Texas. Cookie wasn't there and his mom, working alone, just shrugged her shoulders behind the blue apron.

He wasn't in the front row or any other row. He wasn't at the parties. Sometime the next afternoon his mom phoned. She was crying and said Cookie had called "at nine o'clock last night," as if the important thing was the time of the call. Then she said "he joined the Marines yesterday. He's already there."

In March, on a steaming Sunday morning, Cookie stepped off a path someone else had chosen, walked onto a mine and exploded.

His mother sold the place and disappeared. The new owner changed its name, sold it again, and it shut down. It was empty for years but now it's a bike shop.

My sister swore off boys and started calling herself George. She moved to Canada to work with draft resisters and says she's never coming back. She hasn't yet.

I went to work at the cannery and my income, plus George's "death benefit"–that's a weird-ass term–put Missy through the university. I overdid it once at work and got a nasty hernia for my trouble, but the damn thing kept me out of the army.

Missy's got two degrees but I tell her she can't be as smart as people say, because she's still with me. I'm lucky, and lucky beats smart six ways from Sunday.

She designs playgrounds and I build them, and we do okay. One guy who works for me is from Vietnam and he told me they call it The *American* War. I never thought of that.

Last spring Missy and I went to Washington for the first time. It's been a while since the fall of Saigon, followed soon by the fall of Richard Nixon, but young men are almost always marching and shooting and dying in the name of something that just might be oil, might be patriotism. We touched their names with our hands, our two Georges among the fifty thousand. For a moment it was the way church is supposed to feel.

Cafè Los Cuiles

Her dimples arrived almost before the little girl herself and when she came in through the front door, the beads clicking to announce her arrival, her smile and eyes lit up the dark café.

Open the curtains, we called, Luis and Ita and Lety and I, from our usual corner, and it was done. The new waiter, whose name we did not yet know, did the deed, and we thanked him as he passed us on his way back to the kitchen.

This Oaxacan morning, the day after Christmas, was growing sunny, and the rays painted thin lines on the walls. I thought of walking up the steps to *Cerro Fortin* and the viewpoint near the Benito Juarez statue. I hadn't been there in months and it would be a good day to go.

The girl is four years old, or possibly five, with pink tennis shoes and new blue jeans. Silver stars on her pink shirt spell the name "Dora." What awaits her in the years ahead? She carries the promise of a grand life, a world and future impossible to imagine.

And for us, the regular customers, at our regular little tables, with our coffee, or chocolate, and our bread, who knows? What is to become of us, we who once were young.

Who can say? And more, do I really want to know? I decide that I don't and I stand and leave my share of pesos on the tablecloth. Like the Irish poet I will arise and go now.

I will climb the hill alone today. As long as I can walk, I will walk. Tomorrow, if it be granted to me, I will see my friends again at our café.

Two Days From the Sea

Nothing ever good comes from envelopes with windows. The table once had a surface but the windows were clean once, too. Things change quickly in the fall. It's hard to believe we had a spring this year but it had to be so. Calendars, especially those on refrigerators, do not lie. That's for people.

Six months ago we celebrated three years on the mountain, three years of 4,000 feet above sea-level, though the nearest saltwater is a two-day drive away. Still, nice to think about the ocean as you are high above the desert. We called the house "The Guest House" though we rarely had visitors. It was from a Rumi poem:

"This being human is a guest house.
Every morning a new arrival."

Additionally, indubitably, we knew we, too, were temporary, temporary in the grand scale of existence, and, more to the point, fleeting for each other. In retrospect, three years was longer than either of us would have guessed. Had there been an over-under, we would have lost. Instead, we won, somehow making it work from one spring to the next, and the next, and the next. The house had something to do with it, giving us both space and intimacy as needed, along with the daily cloud pirouettes to the north and east, and the whispers of sunsets in the west.

I did long-distance bookkeeping for three clients. Not many hours required, and little money received, but I didn't need much. My monthly income paid the few bills we had. Wally's early-retirement got us the house. Two men, astride a hill that had snagged itself a mountain name: *Mt. Coronado.* Looking back, it was about the same time as that movie but we were not cowboys, never had been, and never would be.

Wally painted, not for money, though he could have marketed them. I suggested it more than once, but more than twice I did not dare. He said he'd loved all things paint since he was five, the smell, the texture, the mess, the light, and he refused to let the taint of commerce get anywhere near his canvas. Fair enough. He painted, hung, burned, repeated. As I said, we had what we needed, and how many of us can say that. How many of us recognize it, much less say it?

This spring Wally made the two-day drive to the coast, to be with his brothers, to honor his mother, to make a family donation in her name to the hospice she had founded so many years before. Ordinarily, if one of us went west, we both did, but I'd been ill much of that winter, and though I felt fine by March, we both knew the best place for me was our sun-filled rock garden. We also knew his brothers and I were never going to be buddies and there was no reason to dance that dance again.

Wally stayed away an extra few days, for "family stuff," which was not unusual. When he did return, the Toyota pick-up kicking up dust on our dirt road a full three minutes before he reached the house, I welcomed him with warm coffee and a warmer kiss. I told him about the nothing he'd missed by not being here. In return he didn't tell me about his visit to his ancient family doctor to learn that he, not the ancient physician, was quickly dying. It was the spring that Wally learned–I did not learn until September–how well he could lie, even to the one he loved. He always was talented.

Junk mail urges me to buy life insurance. Too little, too late. And it's just another lie, too, isn't it.

At Last

It was around two in the afternoon, on the way back from Spring Green to Madison, when the sky blackened, just like that. Faster than just like that. One minute it was blue skies and sunny, and the next he couldn't see ten feet in front of him. The van on the two-lane farmland highway was pounded and buffeted by wind and rain. He could have been inside a bass drum. He pulled over, terrified of driving off the concrete and down into a ditch. At times he could see nothing, at other times he saw less. He didn't remember what the side of the road had looked like before the storm.

He was wearing jeans and a "Mad City" t-shirt, purchased the day before for a quarter from a garage sale or tag sale or yard sale, whatever they called them in this state. So it was a t-shirt day, and his dusty sandals, as the morning had started out pretty warm. The drive along Highway 14 had been a golden mesh of late summer and early fall. Now he was cold and he didn't think he was on 14 anymore.

There hadn't been much traffic to begin with, and that was before the storm. As he waited a pick-up truck passed, then two cars, and the second car pulled over to the right maybe thirty yards ahead of him. Now that car, like his, was motionless, only the emergency lights flashing. After a long five minutes, or ten minutes—it was hard to say, the other car pulled back into the eastbound lane, and disappeared. Robby was scared to stay and scared to go. As faint as the other car's flashers had been, he didn't know if people would see his in time, or even if he were pulled over far enough. He desperately wanted to get off the highway but was terrified of driving any further at all where the wipers could not compete. How long was it going to last? Was it safer here, sitting and cringing every time a vehicle neared, or getting back into traffic and driving blind? Safety was not possible. All choices were danger, could be fatal. He thought, without irony, without drama: "this could be where and how I die."

He'd only gone to Spring Green and the Frank Lloyd Wright thing to please his mother. She'd made him promise that if he got within 100 miles of it, he must go, for her. Among the many mysteries that made up his mom, her fascination for Wright and his designs was high on the list. She otherwise had no interest in architecture, worked as a beautician, and lived in a nondescript Fresno tract home. But, she had asked, and he had gone. From the tourist shop inside the center he'd mailed her a postcard–they were no dummies, they sold stamps, too, and had their own mailbox–to prove he had done it. The tour had been okay but he really didn't care about it, and felt a little guilty that he was somehow taking the space of some architecture student somewhere who really would have loved to be there. As he strolled the grounds he imagined Jake back in Madison, no doubt getting some local action. He had already made the acquaintance of a radical feminist, but likely not so radical that he didn't have a chance. That's the way it was–Jake scored, and he sent postcards to his mom.

After another timeless stretch he braved driving again. Maybe it had let up the slightest bit, or he had gotten used to it, or maybe it was just desperation and an unwillingness to do nothing. He drove cautiously–if elderly ants were on the road today they were keeping up with him–flashers on, for a couple of miles. He saw a sign and could barely make it out, but it indicated an exit to "Barnevald." He didn't know it, and hadn't noticed it coming out, so it couldn't be too big, and the sign didn't say how far it was. He didn't know how far he was from Madison but it was going to be longer getting back than it had been coming out, that was the only clear thing around. He turned at the exit. Could it be just a mile, or was it five, or ten? Who knew? Was anything there? He wanted so badly to get out of the car. Anything public, a gas station, a restaurant, a drug store…a police station would be great. Even though the storm wasn't likely to last at this intensity for hours and hours, he thought of splurging on a motel room and hiding there, if it had power, until it was over, even if it meant spending the night, and no matter about the money. He could afford a Motel 6, even a Ten or Twelve.

The road was broader somehow, though that made no sense. It had to be smaller than the highway and the highway hadn't been super-

wide. But it was going north instead of east, or east instead of south–
he really wasn't sure–and he could see more, too. Much more. The
road rolled gently away from the horrible highway and that alone was
calming. At the same time, he feared to wander on a tiny road going
nowhere, toward an unknown town of no known location, no known
services. Now a new sign promised: "Barnevald–one mile." He
exhaled. He could do another mile.

Barnevald, the following sign showed, had a bit more than 1,000
people. Would there be anything for him? The rain still rattled and
roared. He didn't see a gas station, but he saw a market, with lights on,
and pulled in and parked in the almost empty lot. He turned the motor
off, put the key in his pocket, and sat for a while, attempting to ease
his heart, his mind, his body, and his soul if he had one. He no longer
feared death but he was still sweating. He opened the driver's door
against the storm's power and ran from the car to the store's door. It
took only seconds but he was soaked and shivering, clothes drenched,
by the time he made it. It was bigger inside than he would have
guessed, three or four aisles, even a café-area with two small tables,
probably for sandwiches or coffee. He saw two workers who probably
hadn't seen much business today, and who were going about the
chores you do on slow days. One woman was standing at the register,
and a second woman appeared and disappeared near the back. Later he
noticed a bread man, arranging loaves on a rack near the tables. He
must have been out driving, too.

The first woman greeted him, but he could hardly respond, unless
shaking was communication. He asked if he could just stay inside for a
bit because the storm was so strong.

"Sure, honey, stay as long as you want. We're open 'til six."

She came to where he was standing and they looked out the glass
doors to the pelting rain and the water streaming down the road. The
noise was a freight train, and when the thunder cracked, it could have
been bombs exploding in the next block. Soon she returned to her set-
up work at the checkout stand. Robbie said he'd buy something, but he
just needed to catch his breath first, and she said there was no hurry.

He walked the aisles, dripping with each step, then bought donuts and a bottle of water, and sat at one of the tables, but didn't open the donuts or the bottle. He just sat there.

At some point the woman from the back came through and handed him a well-worn Pendleton shirt.

"Here, you can wear this. I don't need it right now."

Imagine a world with such kindness, he thought, and quickly put it on over his thin, wet shirt. His nerves were raw and he was wracked with gratitude.

He sat for forty minutes, nibbling and sipping, and occasionally going to the door to see the wild kingdom outside. At one point he raced out to the van. It was still pouring, but not as hard, and he yanked open the door and grabbed a hooded sweatshirt. He slammed the door shut and hustled back into the store. He was heading for the bathroom in the back, which he had already used once, when he ran into the Pendleton woman. He thanked her again. He had thanked her many different times already, every time she was near, and apologized now for getting it so wet. It was heavy now, just from the quick run to and from the car. She accepted the soggy shirt, assured him it would dry, and he would, too. He used paper-towels to knock off the latest round of rain from his hair, face and hands. Then he put on the sweatshirt. As he looked at himself in the mirror he thought what a nice thing it was to thank someone. If nothing else, you could probably always find a reason to thank somebody.

They told him the storm was supposed to lessen soon, and that it had surprised them, too. "We get these in the summer, but this one is way late."

He found a pre-made sandwich and bought it, along with chips and a coke. He figured that by the time he'd eaten, it would probably be okay to go. He remembered the Spanish word for storm: *una tormenta*. That was on the money. As he unwrapped the sandwich another sopping body walked in.

"Hey there, Michael," said the clerk. Her name was Daisy, Robby had learned earlier, when she had asked for his.

"Daisy, good day to you. And who is this?"

"Robby's a pilgrim passing through, from California I guess, but he's just going up to the capital today."

"Nice day for ducks, right my new friend?"

"Yeah, I'd have to agree."

Michael shook himself like a dog, took off his jacket and hung it on a chair at the other table, and joined him at his table.

Daisy called out: "Coffee, Hon?"

"Bless you, Daisy, yes."

From the back, a radio that may have been on all the time but now was actually audible because of the slight adjustment in the storm, brought an Elvis tune into the mix.

"Coffee for you, too?"

"No thank you, Daisy. My mom says it's too strong for me, and she's right."

"I think we might have some hot chocolate mix in the back. How about that?"

"I'd love that, thanks."

The hot drinks arrived. Now the radio was playing some old stuff, big band stuff like his father used to play, back when his father wanted to be a father. Michael was either an accountant or a skilled impersonator of one, clad in black slacks, black shoes, and white shirt, complete with pencils in the pocket. He might have been 40. He looked back toward the source of the music.

"Do you recognize that?"

"Sort of," he said, "but not as an instrumental. I only know the Etta James version."

"This is where she got it, it's the Glenn Miller Band. Before my time, too, really, but it's a good one. I like it both ways, but maybe this way best. But I heard it first without the words."

He wasn't sure. He liked plenty of instrumentals, old and new, but maybe there was too much empty space in this one. He had to admit some people thought the Etta James vocal was mushy, but not him. In the right circumstances, there would always a place for mush.

"Hey, Daisy," Michael called.

"Yeah, Hon?"

"Okay if I tell him our story?"

She laughed. "If I said no, you'd still tell it, right?"

"Well, not if…not…yeah, I probably would, wouldn't I?"

"I can't think of anyone in town who doesn't know it, and he's fresh blood for you. I won't stand in your way."

"Thank you, sweetie."

Robby dipped a little cookie—a Madeleine?—into his drink. Daisy was a good hostess, for sure, and it looked like she was a good friend, or more, to Michael. If the rain ended up *not* letting up, he suspected he could safely stay the night in this little town, and that was a nice feeling, but he'd rather get back to Madison today.

"I didn't know about that, that it was from Glenn Miller. I'm supposed to know that stuff, too, 'cuz I'm a DJ at my school station."

"All right, that's a good thing. Our little station here is pretty important to us. And my cousin's on right now. He always picks good stuff."

"He is on a roll, that's for sure." The extended set of Ray Charles was an example of that.

"Do you go the university up at Madison?"

"No, I go in Los Angeles, but I'm taking some time off. Me and a friend are just seeing the country for a couple of months. We are crashing in Madison for a couple of days, though."

"I thought that was a California plate out there. We usually have better weather for our visitors this time of year. I'll complain to the mayor."

He laughed. "I'd appreciate that, but don't be too hard on him. Things happen."

"I'll be gentle, and it's a her, not a him." He pointed at Daisy with his thumb.

"Really? That's cool."

"Cool except when people really do blame her for everything. But, yeah, she does a good job."

Daisy came to refill the coffee. She stopped to run her fingers through Michael's hair.

"Getting a little thin on top," she smiled as she spoke, "but no signs of grey. I like that in a man."

"Flattery, flattery. And thank you for the joe, too."

She sat down with them. "Don't know why I'm standing over there. Have either of you seen a paying customer around here? Present company excepted, of course."

She nudged Michael's elbow. "So, did you tell the tale?"

"Coming right up, and you can correct me if I forget anything."

"If you forget anything, I'll faint and won't be any help. Wait just a second, let me go get another hot chocolate. Would you like that?"

"That'd be great. For a while I thought I'd never stop shaking. Thanks again."

They waited until she returned with the new Styrofoam cup. Just putting his hand on it was a pleasure, and the chocolate went down easy, too.

"So it was 1952 and I was shipping out for Korea. Three of us were going in from here, plus a couple from out in the county, and they give us a dance at the Legion Hall, kind of a going-away thing."

"There were ten of you all together, but I don't remember exactly where the other boys were from," Daisy said.

"Yeah, and this little lady was on the refreshments committee. We knew each other, of course. You can see this ain't exactly New York or Milwaukee, but she was just this kinda cute little kid. I mean I was twenty-one, almost twenty-two, and she was barely in high school."

"Excuse me, I was finished with sophomore year already. I was already sixteen."

"Yes, you were, and I was closing in on twenty-two. *And* I'd been going out with your sister for over a year."

He wondered if they remembered he was here.

112

She turned to him. "He *thought* he was seeing my sister but that was a whole 'nother story. Suffice to say she and old Mr. Pickett at the bank were also making some plans."

"We all said 'old Mr. Pickett' but we're both older than him now. Than he was back then."

"Speak for yourself, old man."

"Oops, my error. Excuse me, Princess."

"Anyhow," they said at the same time, then stopped, then laughed. "Okay, okay, it's your story," she said. "I'll be quiet now."

"We'll see about that," Michael grinned. "*Anyhow*, as far as I knew at the time, I had a future with the sister, but that night, for the first time, I really *saw*, really *looked at*, Miss Daisy here. I liked what I saw, too, but, like I said, I was leaving, and I had her sister getting ready to be waiting for me."

"I looked, too," she whispered.

Michael gave her a mock glare and she covered her mouth with her hand. "Shush, now," she said to herself.

"Like you said, 'things happen.' Pretty soon I was in Korea and the first letter I got, was my mom wrote me that Daisy's sister and the banker-man had run off to Minnesota. That's the kind of thing that'll sour a guy on mail call, I'll tell you right now. Funny thing, I'd always kind of pegged him for a fairy. It never bothered me but it was just there, you know. Turned out I was wrong.

"So I take it out on the Commies and chase them up and down the peninsula for a year and then I come back. Now it's been two years total since I was home, thanks to basic training and the strange system the army's got to get you places. I'm proud I served–don't get me wrong–but I'd never recommend it for a travel agency. Evanston, Illinois; Fort Sam Houston, Texas; Fort Lewis, Washington, and I was there before *and* after Texas; and finally Fort Cronkite in your state. You ever been to San Francisco?"

"Oh, yeah," he said, "it's great."

"It was great then, too," Michael recalled, a look in his eyes that apparently caused some alarm in Daisy, so she slapped him, ever-so-gently, on his right hand.

"But what happened in Frisco, stays in Frisco," he said, employing a phrase he'd clearly used before. "Anyway, Army HQ wouldn't know a straight line if one stood up and punched 'em in the nose. The single solitary time they have you going straight is when you are marching. Otherwise they just spin the compass and send you on your way."

Bells jangled and all three looked to the door. A dark man in white pants and a white jacket was pushing a dolly packed with milk crates.

"Riley!" Michael was up and moving toward him. "Need a hand?"

"That would help a lot, thanks. It's slackened, but it's still blowing every which way."

"Can I help?" asked Robby.

"Sure," said Michael, "follow me."

They bundled as best they could and ran out. By then Riley was back outside by his truck. "It's already organized, just hand me boxes from that pile in front, then that one, etc., you know."

Quickly the job was done, three dolly-loads total had made it from truck to store, and Daisy and Riley were arranging the milk and other products in the coolers. As they finished, a couple of "real" customers arrived and Daisy returned to the front. Riley came to the table carrying three ice-cream sandwiches.

"Well, then, have a seat," said Michael. "Riley, this is Robby Jefferson. He's a hippie. Robby, this is Riley–shit, this is Riley *Jefferson*! How 'bout that. Riley's a black man, too. Man, we practically got the Mod Squad today."

"Thanks for your help, man. You must be the California plates."

"That's me. This ice-cream is pretty good pay for five minutes of work."

"Wet work," Michael interjected, "don't forget that part."

"You can have two if you want," Riley told him. "Just tell that cute lady I said it was okay."

"I tell her things are okay all the time, but she don't always listen." Michael pulled up his left sleeve as he said this and Robby saw that he was missing the tips of two fingers on his left hand. Korea? Farming? Accounting?

"Rain's just about done for," said Riley. "That was no fun out there."

"Our man Robby–hey, are you guys related?–got caught in it even before I got here. Daisy said he looked like something the cat dragged in."

She heard that, apparently, because she called over: "Remember, some cats got good taste." He liked the sound of that.

"So, I'm carrying my discharge papers and I'm going this way and that way on this bus line and that one, and I get back to town and it's a Saturday night. The Army had said I wouldn't be leaving base for another month but all of a sudden somebody give me a ticket out of Fort Lewis–third time I was there–and that's how I got ahead of schedule. I figure that's fine, I know my mom will be glad to see me and if I show up early maybe she won't have time to put a banner up or anything."

"I believe I've heard this story before," Riley winked across the table. "But," to Michael, "carry on, please."

"I'll do that. It was Saturday, I said, and I got a ride from Beloit. I coulda waited for a bus the next morning but I ran into old Al Sinor and his big Dodge, and that's how I got home. And don't you know, we come up on the Legion Hall and it was obvious something was going on inside. We stopped right there."

Daisy had appeared out of nowhere and picked up the story: "He walked into the dance hall and the moon was shining in the doorway behind him. It was like Marshal Dillon or John Wayne walking into a saloon. He looked good in that uniform, too."

"I couldn't looked too good, I'd been wearing it for 'bout four days straight."

"Trust me, you looked good."

115

"And I look acrost and I barely recognize you. You was all growed-up and beautiful as could be. 'Course, it had been a long time since I'd seen a woman up close."

Another gentle slap.

"And, God love him, Al Sinor goes up to the guy playing the records and tells him to play 'At Last.' I looked over at him and he winked at me, and then I looked back here at Daisy and walked right up to her. I ain't stopped looking since."

The audience applauded as the hero and heroine held hands and she gave him a kiss on the cheek.

"I was reading another book about Thomas Jefferson," Riley said, nodding to him. "We may well be family. Your side got any money?"

"I was just gonna ask you the same thing."

"Oh, well. Look, I'm heading out, back toward Madison. It'll be easier for you now, for sure, but if you want to follow me, it'll be even better."

"Great idea, thanks."

All four stood from the table. Daisy gave cheek-kisses to both travelers, and Michael shook his right hand hard, and held it for a while, holding his gaze, too. "You take care of yourself."

"You too, both of you. I'm grateful to you."

Daisy and Michael followed them to the door, Michael's left hand locked tight with her right. The rain had completely stopped but he kept close behind the truck until it pulled off with a honking version of "shave and a haircut, two bits," just west of Madison.

There was no sign of rain. He thought he remembered where that used record store was, the one they had discovered yesterday. He'd search the bins for an Etta James cassette. He imagined listening to it once or twice a day for the rest of the trip. There could be storms.

"No, I used to have long hair like yours. Longer. But then I got it cut because I had to, you know." The second man joined him: "*get a job.*"

"I do yardwork," added the second man, "so it never made any difference."

The man who no longer had long hair was sitting in the last seat on the train, sketching on a Strathmore drawing pad. His rapid strokes suggested he knew what he was doing. The man with long hair stood just behind him although most of the seats were empty. His shoulders rested high against the door.

I hadn't caught the beginning of their conversation but I hadn't missed much, because the long-haired man and I had been outside waiting for that train just a few moments earlier. In the low afternoon sun I'd seen in his face what I myself would have become, had I not, years ago, ceased my cravings for all manner of intoxicants. If he had quit once or twice, as everyone generally did, I had little doubt that his last quitting was a long time passing, and not even a memory now. I suspected he was close to my age but his face was a bad ten years beyond. He towered over me, chalk-skinned and gaunt. He dumped four or five bags—flight bags, duffel bag, canvas bag—on the pavement in front of our bench, and sat down according to a law as strong as gravity, at the far end of the bench.

After five minutes of neutral silence, he muttered: "watch my back," and ambled toward the shrubs at the north end of the platform. I assumed he was asking or telling me to keep an eye on his stuff. Possibly he had said "watch my bags," but I think he just put the two phrases together. I remembered the time a client told me that "the hand was writing on the wall" and it was hours before I realized what he was talking about. Back at the station I just figured this man had a sudden need to urinate, and everybody knew the restrooms were locked tight on weekends.

But when he returned he was clutching a fair approximation of a bouquet, culled from the meager offerings available in the sparse landscaping. He sat again, pulled out a phone, and called someone named "Babe." He told Babe he'd be leaving Palo Alto at 5:29, so "just jump on the train in Millbrae." After a pause, he continued: "Just get on the first one after 5:29...No, I'm not getting off, I'll be *on* it...We will *not* miss each other, because I won't get off. I'll be all the way in the back...No, not much. But I have enough...Okay, see you soon. You're ready, right?"

"We're going to Oregon tonight," he said. His phone was shut now so if he were speaking to anybody, I was the one. "We'll take all this to the city, then bust ass over to Greyhound for the 7:40 to Oregon. We're gonna stay there for sure. We've had about enough of this place. Too much history. Way too much drama. If it's close, I'll pay for a taxi to get to Greyhound. Can't miss that bus because the next one has a five hour layover somewhere."

Fooled again. I peered at this stringy-haired romantic with bad teeth and a Northern California history I could recite in my sleep and be ninety percent accurate. But it was the ten percent that I was always getting wrong, when I slapped my labels on someone and thought I knew all there was to know.

We returned to our books—mine was a thin Penguin paperback, a P.G. Wodehouse farce bustling with butlers and artistes and young lovers. I bought it for all of three dollars in Know Knew Books across from my office, my treat to myself for going in on a Saturday, and I almost laughed out loud at one point, but before I could, *he* did. A few moments later, he laughed again. Was he reading his own book or looking over my shoulder? My book *was* as funny as anything I'd read in months, but I still couldn't imagine that this guy would see it the same way. I looked over. It was his book that had him going, an oversized hardback on the San Francisco 49ers. He turned to me.

"You should read this! You a football fan? Man, I can't wait until the real season starts again. This book is great. Why can't they play one exhibition or practice game, or whatever the hell they want to call it, every week, all year, until the regular season? Hell, I don't care who's in the uniforms, high school kids, scrubs, it don't matter. I just like to watch. You a football fan? This book cracks me up." A small flat bottle materialized. "Hey, you want some?"

"No," I said. "Thanks, though." He took the smallest sip possible. The bottle disappeared into a jacket pocket and we resumed our reading but Jeeves kept getting tackled by Matt Hazeltine and Leo Nomellini, 49ers from my childhood, from, from, no, could that be right? I watched those guys on a rabbit-eared black and white television, and five times in person, forty years ago. More. When was the last time I'd thought about those heroes, and that one season of Sundays that we walked through Golden Gate Park to Kezar Stadium, my father, my grandfather, and me? This guy's football book wasn't doing my British drawing room comedy any favors, but I welcomed the nostalgia. Those stadium benches were a lot like this backless bench, and I stood to loosen my stiff body.

The train, our train, arrived. Saturday is not a big day on the commuter line so you wait a long time, almost two hours in our case. We boarded through different doors but I found myself moving toward the back where he was standing, perched over the artist.

"Get a job!"

I eased into a seat that faced the rear of the car, the artist, and the daisy-grasping shadow of the sixties—we probably saw Hendrix on the same nights—his menagerie of bags again resting in a clump, and then, as if a master-switch had been flipped, his face burst into an extravagant, crooked-teethed grin. You don't often witness a brainstorm, but that's what I saw.

"Hey, in a couple of stops my girlfriend's getting on. See these flowers? She's a beautiful black woman with the coolest hair you've ever seen. Listen. How about if you draw her for me? Would you do that? I'd pay you—and she wouldn't even know about it until it's finished! God, that would be great! Would you? What would it cost? I've got the money. Ten? Twenty? I've got the money. We're going to Oregon."

Even as the artist smiled with a "sure, man, no problem, glad to," another guy across the aisle offered up his seat. "You and your girlfriend should sit here, where he can see her, and she'd have no idea." "Wow, thanks, man, that is perfect." The donor took a new seat, staying close to the stage he'd set.

"Here, I'll sit over here, where he was, and when she comes, I'll make her sit across from me, so you'll have a good look at her. God, she's beautiful. She says I look like Dracula. Once she said 'what am I doing with a white man who looks like a *dead* white man?' But I tell her she's gorgeous. And she is. Remember, we won't say anything–we'll act like we just met — hey, we *did* just meet. What's your name, man? I'm Victor. Then, when you're done, you'll give it to me, and I'll give it to her. And I'll pay you, too."

We waited. One stop. Two stops. Which stop was it? He'd told me, but I couldn't remember, and I was getting nervous. He was mellow, chattering with the artist about the Oregon trip, about his girlfriend, about the folly of cutting perfectly good hair to get a job, but with each stop I wasn't so sure. I'd heard his end of the phone conversation so I was reasonably sure she existed, but you never know. And even if she did exist, would she get to her station on time? Did she really want to? Was she on the same page?

The stops kept coming.

"There she is. Just act natural." At his instructions the artist promptly looked out the window. The other guy raised a crumpled Chronicle. She reached the back of the car.

"Hello young lady, don't I know you?"

"Well, I don't think so," said a tall dark-skinned woman with braids in all directions.

I'd been afraid to look at her because I didn't want to be the one to ruin things. I had to laugh at myself, since nobody else knew that I knew, but I was excited. I wished I'd seen her face.

"I think you might be a friend of a sister of a cousin of mine."

"No sir, you're wrong, but I'll take a chance and sit next to you anyway."

"Ahh, no, sit across from me, so I can figure out where I know you from. Besides, you're one sweet vision in a sour world, and this way I can gaze upon you all the way to San Fran. Does your mama know where you are?"

"My mama is a million miles away, so you don't need to worry about her."

"Well wherever she is, she's got one fine-looking daughter. You can take that to the bank and live on it for a month. How about letting me try on those shades of yours, they hide too much of your face. Hey, look what I have, pretty flowers for you."

"You're a sweet talker, mister. You can charm the glasses right off me, and maybe a whole lot more. You are one dangerous man."

She released her two suitcases and situated herself where he, where all of us, willed her to be. I watched the exchange of dark glasses and white daisies. Across the aisle, the artist shifted slightly and made graceful swoops with his pencil. Bits of conversation reached me but now it was mostly whispers. The artist continued to work as the conductor called 22nd Street, my refuge for the next thirty-six hours. The trail from the tracks to my own love's door took exactly nine minutes when I walked quickly and we hadn't touched in ten days and ten nights; still, it was with hesitant steps that I crossed the tracks and headed east.

She hugged me, had seen me coming, had run to the gate. *"Besame mucho,"* her throatiest voice, *"como la primera vez." Kiss me deeply, like the first time,* she crooned the classic ranchero lyrics we both mocked and treasured, and we did, we kissed to make up for lost time, our hug turning into a grinding embrace, outside in the still warm evening, beneath the lone eucalyptus that filled her yard. When we reached her door, our shirts pulled out and my fingers already tugging at the snaps on her blue jeans, I managed to say: "I should have brought flowers, but I did bring a story."

Johnny on the Spot

We had met five times, maybe more, in the little attorney room out at the old jail. He was neither smart nor stupid, just your basic messed-up nineteen-year old, but he was locked-up and charged with Attempted Murder, facing a maximum of nine years in prison. More likely, if he was good for it at all, it would be a lesser charge of Assault with a Deadly Weapon, which carried a four year max. He and three of his buddies had been arrested a few days after a shooting in the park that runs along the dry riverbed. No one had died; in fact, the only one who got hit was out of the hospital in twenty-four hours.

In the jail everyone wore orange jumpsuits. No red, no blue, no vivid reminders of alliances on the street. Not that all the inmates didn't know who was who and what was what, but the colorful shirts, caps and bandanas were left behind in "prisoners' belongings," to be retrieved if and when their owners were released.

Johnny was likeable enough. He even had a job waiting for him on the outside, driving a truck for the Sofas So Good on Market Street. And given that neither he nor his pals could shoot for shit–if they were the guys who'd done the shooting at all, which they probably were–he wouldn't be in forever. The question to be determined at trial was this: did he shoot or was he merely an accomplice. And if he were an actual shooter, was he the one who clipped the sole victim. We probably couldn't convince the jury that he wasn't there at all so the next best thing was that he was there, yes, but that's all, and his pals did all the shooting. In California, accomplices get slammed, too, but you don't want to go down as a shooter. Judges don't like people who shoot at, and hit, other people, even if the other people are punks or thugs or gang-bangers.

We don't usually have our clients testify but for this one I'd need to put him on the stand. He'd made some statements to the cops and the jury was going to hear them whether he testified or not, so he needed to explain some things. Also, he had no prior convictions–a unique status among his friends. And more, he cleaned-up pretty good.

Wearing civilian clothes provided by his mother, he'd be presentable. I was lucky in that regard. The co-defendants looked like they'd been raised for prison. One had the popular teardrop tattoo below his left eye. Another had *fuck you* inked on the back of his neck. His attorney would find him a high-collared shirt but you had to wonder if it wouldn't be visible somehow. Hell, the guy might intentionally tug his shirt down to show everyone how tough he was.

With Johnny, prepping him for testimony came to this, over and over. *Stick to your story—the one you've told me every time. Don't say anything else. Don't say anything you don't know. Don't guess. Don't try to be helpful. Just listen to the questions and be honest. And if you don't know, say you don't know. Be polite, listen to me when I'm asking you questions, but look at the jury. Listen to the prosecutor when she's asking you questions, but look at the jury. They want to believe you.*

It looked like two of the four guys had fired shots. When they were arrested only one had a gun and it wasn't Johnny. The vague descriptions provided by the witnesses–a young mother with two toddlers, a park maintenance man, and one of the "victims"–all suggested that Johnny *probably* wasn't one of the shooters. But that didn't mean he wasn't.

The trial date arrived and we danced through the jury selection shuffle in a mere three days. In a four-defendant case, that's rolling in high gear.

The prosecution commenced and there were no surprises. I've done this a lot the past fifteen years so the lack of surprises was no, well, you know. As I'd figured, our boy would have to testify. If I were a betting man–which I am, just ask the dealers at Artichoke Joe's Casino–I'd say if he didn't totally screw up in the witness box, the jury would convict the other three and let him go. Juries like to throw a bone that way. At worst, he'd pick up an aiding-and-abetting and only a few more months in county. No trip to the state prison for him. If he did his job.

I did my job–it's what I do–asking him questions just as we'd practiced. Sure, the DA would get her turn but I wasn't worried about that. She was limited to the scope of my own questions and the judge would make sure she behaved herself. The jury would figure he was there, but gee, that could happen to anyone, and they'd appreciate his candor. No other defendant would testify. They'd already packed their bags for the joint.

As I finished, just before the obligatory "your witness" hand-off to my opponent, I threw in one last question—an easy one—to leave the jury with a clear denial to carry with them into deliberations.

"So, Johnny, so we are all clear, did you shoot anyone on August 16th last year?"

"I don't know. No, I don't think so."

Johnny's not coming home anytime soon. If there are any young attorneys out there, write this down. Juries don't like ambiguity.

Mother, With Child

Summer sunlight pierced the high windows, angling to catch the dust that floated in the air before coating the ancient hardwood tables. At the longer table, in front of the empty jury box, sat two attorneys, one for the county, and one *from* the county but "for the child," and a third person, a social worker, the three quietly chatting. Sitting opposite them at a smaller table were the client and her attorney. Just below and to the right of the judge's perch, behind a tiny table, was a barely visible stenographer, and, below and to the judge's left, wearing a pistol on his right hip and sunglasses over his eyes, his belly craving escape above his wide black belt, was the bailiff, his surname Newman prominent on his chest. The unquiet silence ended when Newman stood and all came to order and the judge materialized from a door the attorney hadn't even seen. All rose but the one in whose name they were gathered, who remained elsewhere, in the county's children's shelter, the client's fourteen-month daughter: *In the matter of Alondra Cruz.*

The client was nineteen. The attorney was twenty-five, but even dressed in a suit as mature as she could abide, could have passed for twenty. Across the room, each of the county attorneys clearly possessed two to three full decades of adulthood, and the social worker's face suggested similar experience. The judge was beyond age. The client's attorney had never done this before. In fact, she'd never spoken out loud in court without a supervising attorney sitting discreetly at her shoulder, while still a law student, and then, none of her cases had involved a mother desperate for her child.

The client worked in alfalfa fields and with the dairy cows on a farm outside Monroe. At first, her husband's mother watched the child while they both worked, but after the husband and mother-in-law never returned from a funeral in Texas, she'd arranged with neighbors to look after her. The housing was stacked one against another. Everyone knew everyone, and everything about everyone, whether they wanted to or not. Most recently, a large eleven-year old girl had watched the child, but when the mother trudged home two Fridays ago, she found neither baby nor sitter. Four pounding hours later, a deputy sheriff drove up in a shiny green police cruiser. From his car window he explained in increasingly louder and slower English to the mother and to her closest neighbor, who understood more English, that her daughter had been picked up at two in the afternoon, playing alone in the field near the filling station that doubled as the bus stop. The sheriff had no information on the eleven-year old.

That was ten days ago. Today, they were inside the vast courtroom that was the showpiece of the historic town square. The skinny, trembling mother, in her best dress, the one she carried with her when they crossed in March, the dress not as white as it once was, with the faintest hint of blue flowers in a semi-circle at her throat; behind her, alone among the rows of polished benches, the neighbor who spoke a little English, and who, if the court permitted, would be called by the mother's attorney to explain what had happened, as interpreters were provided only in criminal cases, in a dark blue skirt and light blue button-down shirt; and the mother's attorney, who at times clasped her own hands together to keep them from shaking.

It could take all morning, it could take twenty minutes. She didn't know. She had rehearsed what she would say to the judge. Indeed, for three days she'd practiced what she would say to anyone who would listen, and she had also rehearsed, both versions, depending upon the judge's ruling, of what she would say to her client, in her own limited Spanish, after the hearing. As far from fluent in Spanish as she was, she felt a similar and more worrying inadequacy in the language and practice of law. Her white Corvair, once a sassy '66, now almost a dozen years old and as exhausted as an inanimate object could possibly be, was parked outside in front of the coffee shop where she'd spent an eternity waiting for the courthouse doors to open. She had woken at 5:30, arrived outside the courthouse at 6:30, nursed coffee, eggs and home fries until 8:30, and was the first to enter when the courthouse doors opened to the world. Now she waited, drumming the fingers of her left hand on top of her leather briefcase, her graduation gift to herself from the Sacred Feather shop on Madison's State Street. Her right hand rested on her right knee. Her eyes looked only at her two pens aligned next to the yellow legal pads, one completely blank, the other full of the facts and the law, organized as well as she was capable, coded in red and blue ink.

It could take all morning, it could take twenty minutes. She didn't know. How could she know?

Six days earlier, on a sweltering June morning that terminated three years of mind-numbing and distasteful law school classes, she had raised that right hand to be sworn in by the Supreme Court of Wisconsin. By the words of a black-robed justice whose name she had missed, she was now deemed a member of the state bar, a real lawyer. This moment, sitting next to her first client, the silent Anielka Cruz Collazo, was why she endured the three years, why she worked as a waitress and barmaid, why she incurred unfathomable debt, why she jeopardized her own marriage to the point where it jettisoned itself with barely a whimper: to get her ticket to practice. She survived by reminding herself every single day that it was nothing more than a glorified trade school, offering her the only chance she had to get the tools she wanted. This was why. All those years of complaining about the system, the haves and the have-nots, all her dreams of changing the world, or, at a minimum, evening the playing field: This was why.

Exactly twenty-six minutes later, the mother threw her arms around her, sobbing and shuddering so much they both almost fell. Their tears merged. Ninety minutes after that, the now-smiling social worker returned with a timid, then ecstatic, little girl.

She never saw them again. But had she possessed a locket on a silver chain, and had she worn it close to her heart, you would find them. They are always there.

Not Fifth Avenue

It was the pounding of it, more than its liquidity, that demanded my attention, but the rain was sufficiently wet to soak me from head to toe in less than a minute. It wasn't unusual to get "lightning-raid" storms at this time of year, usually around eight in the evening, but this one struck with a power unlike any I'd experienced in my three months in Oaxaca. My jeans and t-shirt were no match for it. Moments ago, I'd been admiring the almost-full moon against the dark sky. Now, I was looking for refuge.

Just yesterday afternoon I'd been on this block, sitting in an *agencia de viajes*, chatting up Cuba with a beautiful young agent named Citlali. My motives were both prurient and practical. She was a stunning sight, her deep green eyes tucked above angelic dark cheeks. "It is pronounced 'Chit-lali,'" she said. "Like chocolate," I either said or thought, and almost forgot why I'd come in. But there also was *Cuba*. Castro had run the place for fifty years and still I hadn't popped in for a visit. I've read dozens of books about it, watched all the documentaries, and grilled anyone I ever met, stranger or friend, who'd actually set foot on the mythical "pearl" of the Caribbean.

I know it as others know Tolkien's *Middle Earth*, Baum's *Oz*, or Shakespeare's *Verona*. For years, I alternated between Fidel and Che at Halloween, depending upon the length of my beard. There are pictures to prove it. From the states it wasn't impossible to get there, but it wasn't easy either, and unauthorized travelers faced real political and financial risks. From Mexico though, I'd heard it wasn't an ordeal, that the prices and packages were good, and that the Cuban authorities were happy to "forget" to stamp your passport, if that was your desire. While I'd love to see such a mark on my passport, my more temperate self did not want a ten thousand dollar fine. I knew a lawyer who had recently developed a sub-specialty of fighting such fines, but I'd rather not play that game.

The lovely Citlali explained various options, showed me prices, pamphlets, and maps. She was intimately versed in all things Cuban, "especially the music," though she also had not yet visited. In her university days, in both Oaxaca and Puebla, while studying Travel and Tourism, and adding a minor in Political History, it had been on her radar, too. I had three more weeks before my return trip to Wisconsin, to the job that rarely excited me and to the home that no longer housed my wife, so I had enough time, and I really did have enough money, but I'd decided to think on it for one more day; sometimes, I do remember that not all of my rash travel decisions have been good ones. Had the vote been called now, just before the rain, I'd have said yes, sign me up, but I was determined to wait until tomorrow, after breakfast, after *pan y chocolate*, before I signed on the dotted line, took a big breath, and paid the cash deposit.

But that was yesterday, not tomorrow. And as luck often had it, today was today. I had been walking about twenty minutes from my apartment on *La Carbonera*, comfortable at first, shivering now. More than shivering, I was shaking. I knew it would pass quickly–most things do–but I could use a respite.

My walk shifted to a jog, then transformed to a splashing run, still heading north, with the thunder caroming between the stucco walls that narrowly lined the cobblestone street. I felt my way along, unable to make out numbers or signs that would confirm I was on the very block of the travel agency. Maybe, *tal vez*, that light up ahead was it, and perhaps, *quizas*, I'd pop in, to get out of the rain, and, who knows, be sheltered by Citlali herself. Now if she were to decide to accompany me to Cuba…oh, my, there was a summer dream to caress. Hell, I'd clutch it to my chest and never let go.

So there was the familiar and inviting door and with two quick hops I was up the steps and inside, dripping like a dog on the immaculate tiled floor. I tried to shake most of it back outside, after which I closed the door and looked around. Looking around is often helpful–to develop a sense of where you are, for example–and it certainly was in this instance because I saw that I was not where I'd thought I was. It was something else, a different office, though of similar dimensions and decor, and someone else sitting behind the counter. Four plastic chairs lined the small office wall. The non-Citlali was speaking softly on the telephone, not looking up. I sat on the end chair, closest to the door and the raindrops I'd brought with me. The two chairs next to me were vacant, with only the last one occupied, by a young woman. Her eyes were half-closed and on her lap was a sleeping little girl.

I almost ventured a *"Buenas Noches,"* but felt constrained not to interrupt her half-sleep. She did acknowledge me with those eyes and a hint of a smile, but did not speak, and re-focused her eyes toward her child. The mom may have been Zapotec, and with my newfound but-still-extremely-limited sense of the various indigenous communities within the State of Oaxaca, I guessed that for her, too, Spanish had been an acquired second language. She was not wearing traditional colorful Zapotec clothing. Instead, she wore the dress of another tradition: modern poverty.

I glanced back at the counter, stuck in that state where you understand you're not where you had expected to be, yet cannot make any sense of how it might have happened. On a tiny side-table I found written documentation of my error, a brochure for this business that included the address. Well, for one thing, I wasn't even on the street I'd thought I'd been. This wasn't *Cinco de Mayo* at all, it was a parallel street, *Los Libres*. This mistake was relatively common for me, especially in Oaxaca, and in itself did not cause any distress. I was still heading in the right direction, toward my friends' place near *Los Arquitos,* for a jovial mix of locals, ex-pats, and in-betweens, not to mention excellent *chocolate caliente.* I wasn't lost, just off a bit. I was laughing a little, internally, I believe, when the woman behind the counter called to the young mother. *"Señorita Nheda, la doctora esta lista."* Ms. Nheda gently raised herself from the chair without waking the child, held her to her chest with both hands, and walked through a now-open door for the doctor who was now ready for her. I returned to the brochure, in no great hurry to go out again, and learned that this doctor was not just any doctor, she was Leticia A. Moreno Flores, *Cardiologia.* And had I been quicker, I would have raced past mother

130

and child, knocking them down if necessary, to seek salve for the sudden piercing in my own heart. Was it the two year-old child or the twenty-year old single mother who required a heart specialist? There was no good answer to that one.

Were this woman, or this child, with me in Cuba, or even back in Janesville, Wisconsin, would the future look better? I couldn't say. I could say, were anyone there to listen, that tonight was drenched in misery.

Through the door I heard a voice, though I couldn't tell if it were the mother's or the clerk's: *"La bolsa."* I now saw the mother's bag was still beside her chair. I sprung to it and shoved in an envelope I pulled from my front pocket, an envelope already filled with twelve five-hundred *peso* bills. I'm no fool, I knew it wouldn't solve everything, and very likely nothing at all, but it might deliver a moment of ease, or, some God grant the small favor, even a little pleasure. I know less and less with each passing summer storm, but I was confident Fidel could do without me for one more year, and with that certainty I began to drag my fortunate self outside for a few more sodden Oaxacan blocks.

Ohio Crossing

Screwed again. Why did she listen to BJ? What did they want with forty wigs anyway? They didn't find any money in the store, couldn't even find the cashbox, so they just stuffed wigs into two big bags and went back out the busted door into the alley. Her first felony. When she admitted it to BJ when they were still inside Columbus city limits trying to get a ride back to BJ's aunt's place, the response was: "It's about time!"

The day wasn't looking good. Zelda leaned on the highway guardrail and kicked the weeds with her red tennis shoes. Their "big score" happened before seven in the morning, and then they'd lugged the stuff a bunch of blocks until they hit a highway entrance. So far they had only the one ride from a smelly old man in an Olds who smoked a cigar and babbled, waving tobacco-stained hands, that he was as old as the century. "I am seventy years young, young ladies. I was born on Independence Day, 1900." He was the strangest since the guys in Pennsylvania who claimed they were federal agents, but he didn't try anything. Drivers usually didn't. The sun was higher now and she was grateful for the heat on her face and shoulders. She didn't know yesterday that they weren't coming back so she hadn't taken a jacket; all she had were her overalls, with undies and a tee-shirt. Two hours ago she was shivering. She kicked herself. Never, ever, go anywhere without your jacket.

If she were home, she'd be in P.E. now, according to her Mickey Mouse wristwatch, which the one good thing her mother ever gave her, not that her mother was the queen of giving.

She hated the locker room and everything in it. Who was cool and who wasn't. Who had bodies and who didn't. She would have flunked it anyway; she rarely dressed out, and never ran even when she did. Forget it. Better a felon than P.E.

BJ shouted and grabbed Zelda's elbow:

"It's stopping! Far out!"

Zelda looked up, then to the right, to a faded red and white VW bus that gingerly backed in their direction, chewing gravel and spitting out the dirt that stretched from the pavement to the barley field on the other side of the fence. She hadn't even seen it go by, but BJ was whispering as it thudded to a stop, "Two guys, two cute guys, I think," whether stating what she'd actually seen, or imploring the gods, Zelda couldn't tell.

A skinny guy with no shirt jumped from the passenger seat and opened the sliding door. He was barefoot and his faded jeans had holes in both knees. You could see the crack of his ass as he picked up their duffel bags and tossed them in the back. BJ hopped onto the little bed in back with the guy and told her to sit up front, so she did.

God, she thought, all she does is order me around. I'm not her little sister. I'm nobody's little sister, least of all BJ's. She stole a glance at the driver before curling up against the passenger door. Robby, they said his name was, and Jake was the guy in back. The driver had leather sandals, blue jeans, and a cool blue corduroy cowboy shirt with pearl snaps up and down and he wore a floppy black cowboy hat. She remembered the Dead song about "Cowboy Neal" and considered calling him Neal. But she didn't. He had a beard, too; the guy in back didn't have any hair on his face. Maybe that meant he was older. He nudged the van back onto the highway but stayed in the slow lane. Good, she thought, what's anybody's hurry? She wasn't going anywhere.

In back, BJ and the guy were already whooping it up, so it was clear where *that* was going. She waited for him to say something about "BJ" and she wasn't disappointed.

Last night was a crummy Columbus apartment with a bunch of jerks. The music was okay but the guys, and it was mostly guys, were drunk and stupid. BJ naturally had a good time, she knew half of the people, but Zelda wasn't in the mood. She'd rather smoke dope than drink any day, and this was mostly drinking. She sat against a wall pretending to watch a non-existent t.v. An older guy started rubbing up against her, just her arm, but it didn't look good, when out of nowhere

BJ appeared and shook her fist at the guy: "Touch her again and I'll bust your face." The guy jumped away in a heartbeat. BJ was all right. BJ winked at Zelda before going back across the room to somebody with an army jacket and bell-bottoms, and nobody bothered her again the whole night. She thought of BJ's tattoo, the dragon on her shoulder, and promised herself again that she would get one, too, a rose, when she got to the coast. A girl at school had a snake twisting between her tits, but she didn't see any point to something like that. Not yet, anyway. She wanted a rose like Janis Joplin. Damn, soon as she hit Frisco, first thing, Janis at *The Fillmore*, and then the tattoo. She could already see it, with her name in cursive, circling the rose. When she got it. One of her names.

Now there was this Neal guy driving. No, not Neal. So many names in this one place. Neal. Robby. Jake. BJ. Funny thing, BJ really was her name, or at least she must be, 'cuz once she heard BJ's crazy aunt holler: "Barbara-Jean Elizabeth!" The guy in back he probably thought it was something she'd earned, like the Scarlet A in that book in Freshman English. And she, how many names did she have now? Zelda. Harper. Alison. BJ sometimes called her "Kid," like she couldn't be bothered with a two-syllable name like Zelda. God, if her mother called her "Birdbrain" once she did it a hundred times. Sometimes, she bet, her mother couldn't remember her real name for a million dollars. Fuck it. She knew who she was, or she would soon, when she got west. She was treading water today, going east again, back to BJ's, but in a couple of days she'd be gone. There was nothing in Ohio; it was just a square on a chalked game of hopscotch between Schenectady and San Francisco. In San Francisco, she would be Harper to some, Zelda to others. And eighteen, and she'd spit in the eye of anyone who said different.

"Pick out something." The driver was pointing to a box on the floor between their seats. Cassettes spilled out of the box. Some were store-bought but most looked to be taped at home. He'd been talking before that, but she didn't know about what. Or how long. She decided to focus. She bent over and pulled the flat wooden crate up to her lap, clicking her way through the plastic cases.

"How about this?" She showed him a case with a hand-written "Then Play On–Fleetwood Mac."

"Good choice. Excellent choice." He removed a tape from the player and traded it for the case she was holding. He slid the new cassette into the machine as she took the old one and dropped it in the box.

"There's never been a case for that one. It's Hendrix: *Are You Experienced*. Damn, Jimi's dead. What a fucking bummer! This bus has heard a whole lot of Hendrix. He was one righteous soul."

As she set the box on the floor she remembered something a guy had said last night, something about Fleetwood Mac. She wasn't a fan but the guy sounded important in the way guys can when they talk about music. She didn't recognize the first song. She reached back again to what the guy, judge-like, had told her.

"They're not going to be the same without…" and here she hesitated. Without? Without what, or who? Paul somebody? Peter? Damn, what was it? A color? How could it be a color?

"…without Peter Green! You are so right on!" Did he have any idea that he, not she, had finished the thought, made the point? She didn't think so. He was looking at her like she was smart, and she blushed. She felt like when they were reading *To Kill a Mockingbird*, and Miss Ogilvie always called on her because she really did know all the answers. She would have got an A if she hadn't caught that cheap case that locked her up in juvie for two months. The father in that book, Atticus, he was a righteous soul, too. Unbelievably perfect, but then, it was a story. She wished she still had the book. But San Francisco probably had bookstores and she was quick with her hands. Jem and Scout were cool names but Harper was better, mature-sounding. She didn't know it was a girl's name until Miss Ogilvie told them. Since she hit the road twenty-two days ago she hadn't told her real name to anyone. She took $140.00 that her mom would kill her for if she ever caught her, which she wouldn't, and she still had most of it. When she

135

met BJ a week ago she just said: "I'm Zelda." BJ claimed to be 18, so Zelda said she was 16.

He looked so happy she decided to talk to him about music. It was easy because he was convinced she knew loads, understood everything he was talking about, and he poured out sentences and paragraphs, barely pausing for her tentative, then more brazen interjections. Turned out you could keep up your end of fifty miles of conversation in a slow-moving van with no more than a rhythm of "Definitely! Right on! Yeah, man! No way!" He was smiling and laughing and that made her happy. He was so quiet at the beginning of the ride. She still stayed way over against her door, she wasn't going to pull a BJ or anything - - God, had she thought that? But it was good to know she could make a guy smile by doing as little as she was. An older guy, too.

"But if I could've seen Clapton before everything exploded, Clapton in some smoky London bar, I could die a happy man. You know, he was only nineteen when he did 'Good Morning Little Schoolgirl?' Did you ever see *Blow Up*? What an amazing movie."

Clapton she knew. Who didn't know Blind Faith? She hadn't seen *Blow Up*, wouldn't have known it was a movie if he hadn't told her.

"Yeah," she ventured, "Eric's cool all right."

"Shit yeah! The Stones are okay, but give me the old Bluesbreakers. I want to feel it, man, I want that beat. That's the best thing about the Beatles, their name."

Zelda returned service. "In school, they all liked Paul but," she paused, prayed, "I was a John fan. It was always John for me. He's the real one."

"Right on!" She'd pleased him again, clearly, and he continued: "He's the brains and soul of that bunch. Big deal that Paul quit. If they do get back together it won't mean a thing unless he's in the mix. Zelda, would you pop that Bluesbreakers' tape in? If you liked that one, wait until what you hear next."

He called her Zelda! She found the tape and made the switch herself. "All Your Love" burst into the van and his right hand tapped the steering wheel. "This. This, my new friend, is the absolute finest piece of recorded music since the first cavemen pounded sticks on rocks."

She laughed, couldn't help it. He turned up the volume, then spoke over it: "Hey, we saw the Dead before we left and we were tripping for days, smoked some *primo* weed that night! We don't carry anything with us, too easy to get pulled over with the California plates. But," his face broke into a broad sun, "if you two happen to be holding, we could maybe find a way to smoke it somewhere, all four of us."

For the first time she felt her body free itself from the metal door. She didn't have anything and she was sure BJ didn't either, but the idea of stopping made her wish they did. She'd practically forgotten about BJ, they must have gone to sleep back there after whatever else they'd done. She started to tell him they were out but maybe they could stop for a hamburger when a scream ruined everything.

"Zelda, that's our turn! That's Coshocton! Pay attention, Kid." She could have ridden for hours, she didn't know where they were.

It wasn't like she saw herself doing it, as if from above or outside her body, but it wasn't like real time either. In the quiet of the stilled van, dirt floating forward from the rear tires, the guitar silenced by the engine-killing turn of the key, she scooted over, seized his face with her left hand, and forced her tongue into his mouth. She swirled it as much as she could, then she pulled away, her teeth catching on his lip, and she tasted blood and without a word...with a word? Had she said something that already she didn't remember? Yes, She had told him her name. Not Harper. Not Zelda. Her real name. Alison.

Standing on the ground, waving with that same left hand at the disappearing van, she opened her right hand, thinking to straighten her overalls strap, and discovered the Bluesbreakers tape.

Hunger

Jenny falls asleep mid-murmur while my eyes trace the ceiling shadows. Her body curves outward from mine. Under her pillow, our left hands join. Her other hand, the only uncovered part of her, ventures a few inches into the night. Her socked feet tuck themselves between my bare ones. My right hand cups her right breast. More often than I prefer, this particular posture calls back a question from a dozen years ago.

Taylor and I had been a couple for six months. People loved us because Octavia Taylor detested her first name, had responded to nothing but "Taylor" from the day she turned eighteen, and my name is Taylor Trzcinski. We had been urged for months to get together. "Come on, it would be so cool! Taylor and Taylor!" We succumbed after a mad daiquiri party in March. It wasn't half-bad. It was so far from half-bad that I dared not question my good fortune.

Taylor needed ten more units to graduate but I had bagged my degree the prior June, celebrating the occasion by cavalierly skipping the ceremony, an act for which my parents, the most forgiving souls in the world, never forgave me. I worked in an off-campus sandwich joint, but expended more of my energy playing fast-pitch softball, and still more vainly trying to organize our players to get to the right diamond at the right time. I was the captain because no one else would be. We were a cheerful bunch on those days we did field a full team, our outfielders serenading our infielders with "Take Me Out to the Ball Game." As long as we had nine players, singing or not, I was content.

Naturally, the one time everybody showed up at my place one hour early, as I had begged them to do for weeks, was the morning after the daiquiri bash.

"Hey Taylor." A pause. Giggles. Then, "Oh, hey to you, too, Taylor," and "Taylor and Taylor, it's about fucking time." One boisterous ballplayer after another opened and loudly shut the always unlocked back door, walked through the kitchen to the curtained doorway to the garage, which was now not a garage but my bedroom, and entered once again. We weren't caught in the act–in fact, we'd been blissfully, and exhaustedly, asleep until the first of the back door slams. We presented a peaceful scene, but the shirts, underwear and blue jeans flung to the corners testified to the passion of the night.

"Hey, Taylor...*Oh, hey*! Hey, hey, hey to you, too, Taylor." She-Taylor knew maybe one-third of the team, but to a man they trooped in, finding spots on or right beside the bed. Taylor, sleepy and bemused and radiant, her red-brown curls tumbling to her shoulders, prudently used one hand to hold the sheet up to her chin, and with the other carefully shook hands with those she hadn't yet met as they gallantly introduced themselves.

"Hello, Rocky, pitcher; Howdy, Ed, second base; Hi, I'm Little Ed, catcher and relief pitcher; Henry, shortstop; Morning, nice to meet you, I play center...my name is Jose."

We were to wake up together in that bed most days for the next two years. Never again was I required to share my first look. She was a morning delight.

The small house was in a cheap sunny section of West L.A., with an alley running behind. A tall stucco wall, with a similarly tall solid gate, separated our backyard from the alley, as well as from the neighbors to either side. The yard itself was nothing but concrete and we parked our semi-reliable cars there. The real bedrooms were occupied by Billy, who was my left fielder and best buddy, and by Eric, who was neither a player nor interested in becoming one. His dream was to be a session sax player, and he wasn't crazy to think so. I didn't see him that much because he worked graveyard for a carpet cleaning company. Billy also played music, an acoustic guitar he had built himself, and was doing temp work at the post office. I played the stereo. Three young men with freshly-printed Bachelor's Degrees of Liberal Arts.

One morning, Taylor, Billy and I discovered three Springsteen t-shirts on the kitchen table, with a note from Eric affirming that they were ours to keep, souvenirs from his night on the job. Neither our degrees nor Taylor's almost-degree status (Human Psychology) had instilled a sense of ethics sufficient to prevent us from swooping them up as our entitlement. Eric had cleaned up at a recording studio in Hollywood. He never did that again, although it is true he didn't keep that job very long. He soon returned to school for a teaching credential and has taught music and history for years.

We all loved Springsteen's music, but the shirts showcased his mythically chiseled face. I wasn't a man to appreciate the beauty of other men but Bruce was an exception. As a girl at work moaned, "God, those orgasmic eyes." Actually, the only man I knew in person remotely worth looking at was Billy. He had wise green eyes, chaotic hair, a bushy mustache that positively bragged about itself, and a grin to charm the jaded of all ages. I once confessed to Taylor that were I ever to unleash any deep-seated gay tendencies, it would be Billy in a heartbeat. Assuming Springsteen was out of town.

Most nights Eric was out working and it was "Billy and the Taylors" hanging out in our small living room. We'd smoke a little dope, solve the problems of the world, watch grainy television, and sometimes listen to Billy and his guitar. Before Taylor moved in, we three guys had lived together almost a year. For six of those weeks Billy had his own roommate, Andrea, in a relationship each knew to be temporary, but the alacrity of its collapse surprised everyone when a real-life professional football player caught her eye, and then the rest of her.

In a way, especially before the advent of Taylor, I suffered Andrea's loss as much as Billy did. In our back cement yard, with the gate closed, we had a perfectly secluded private patio. In addition to the cars, there were two rusted chaise lounges. Andrea, who was between semesters, waited tables at night in a Marina Del Rey restaurant that the rest of us couldn't afford to visit, and couldn't dress the part anyway. She slept until noon and then spent the afternoons reading and working on her tan. It was a warm September, the cracked concrete almost impossible for bare feet. Equipped with sandals and a novel, a pink bikini bottom and a large iced tea, Andrea settled on one of the lounges on a beach towel emblazoned *Acapulco*. I followed in sandals and cutoffs, with my own book and beer, to the other lounge. She was happy for my company, though she teased me for my motives: "you probably don't even like the sun, you're really just a tit man, aren't you." When she said that, I would protest, noting that "the sun was big enough for both of us, and the light was good for reading, too."

She was right. She was the reason I was outside. But it wasn't her body, its size, or shape, or anything unique that enthralled me. I saw them as normal breasts, nothing special. Older, I've learned to treasure all working anatomy, all types, understand that all are special and temporary. Age has a way of concentrating the mind. I didn't mind seeing her topless, certainly, but I wasn't craving, or hungering, or anything like that. It was just that when the sun's rays were peaking, I could not resist doing a little peeking of my own, to savor the tiny pool of glistening sweat that settled just between them. That's what I wanted. I am still struck by that perfect sensuality.

Out our front door, which was almost never used, was the backyard of the landlords, whose house faced the street. The Riveras were non-intrusive, content with our always on-time, in-person, rent check, and otherwise left us alone. They also rented the back room of their home to Peggy, a single mother, and her three-year old daughter, Molly. We got to know Peggy and Molly a little after Taylor joined our household. We knew no one else with a child, so Peggy was an anomaly and Molly a complete novelty. The Riveras, childless and in their fifties, sometimes looked after Molly in the evenings after Peggy brought her home from day care on campus. It was ideal for Peggy who was constantly working late in the lab. She was finishing a postdoctoral in something involving micro-bio stuff. She tried to explain it to us once but we were hopeless.

Peggy ignored what the old right-hander Satchel Paige called "the social ramble," and if she ever smelled the marijuana, she never came by to join in. She was from England, which made her wonderfully intriguing to us, and she wore her hair like Marianne Faithful did a long time ago. When she laughed, which wasn't often, I noticed an overbite.

No one in our house was a fashion plate but even we could see how drably she dressed. Her priorities, and money, went to the basics for her daughter, and then her research. There was nothing, and no one, for her.

If an absent father existed, we never saw him. Once, Taylor told me what Peggy had said, that Molly's father disappeared when Peggy got pregnant. And, Peggy had told Taylor, "He wasn't all that much anyway." Taylor was privy to another fact: Peggy had been with a man just once since Molly had arrived, and that had been "for about ten minutes." Everyone in our house was twenty-two years old. Peggy had to be close to thirty.

The night that returns this night, returning as real as the sense memory I get when I bite into fudge that isn't even half as good as my grandmother's ever was, that comes back to me while my sweet Jenny rests safely in my arms, was one of those typical nights in that little house, with the three of us mellow in the tiny rectangle of a living room, poor Eric off somewhere cleaning carpets. I distinctly recall Billy on the floor with his guitar. Taylor was sitting on the couch. I lay sprawled half-off the couch with my head in her lap. The front-door knock was a surprise—everyone used the alley. Who could it be but the landlords or Peggy, though at close to eleven either was hard to imagine. Peggy it was, and when she closed the door behind her, I saw that though she was cold sober, her face radiated with color.

She perched on the stuffed chair we'd rescued from a sidewalk, her back a good foot from its torn upholstery. Balanced just so, she took a few breaths.

"I've come for a favor." She paused. "Goodness, I sound rather as if I were here to borrow a cup of sugar, but that's not it. But I do need something."

"No problem," I said. "Our casa is *su casa*. What can we do? A bottle of wine? A joint? A softball?"

She laughed a quick two seconds, then stopped. "Well, I need...will you...oh, it was much easier in the car."

"Go on. Baby-sitting? We'd love to do that! Anything you need, we're here to help."

"Very well. I'll ask. *I have to ask.* Billy. Billy, will you make love to me tonight? Now?"

The guitar shrieked, then shut down. I sat up, holding Taylor's hand. I was sitting so straight my shoulders hurt. Billy didn't budge. Silence swept in from the four corners, filling all available space. Peggy broke it.

"I'm asking a lot, I know, but in a way, maybe not so much? I'm not so terrible, am I? I'm completely scrubbed and lotioned."

"This is weird." Billy's voice came from a new place. "I mean, I like you fine, but…" I waited. After thirty seconds that felt like a month, Peggy tried again.

"It is unusual. Of course I know that, but when you think about it, where's any real objection? We're both adults. You are a lovely man." She smiled at me. "Taylor, you are adorable, too, but you're taken."

"You bet he is," from my Taylor.

"And," spoken more to the room than to any one person in it: "I'm not, what is that darling expression, I'm not somebody you would 'kick out of bed.' I'm not, am I?"

She wasn't, but nobody said a word. She was on the chair, Taylor and I ramrod straight on the couch and Billy still on the floor, struggling to quiet his guitar as if it were a restless dog. I was conscious of a rhythm from down the little hall and realized it must be the ticking of Eric's alarm clock, though I'd never heard it out here before.

I don't remember the weather that night but I was sweating. The room shrunk smaller than usual. Peggy's gaze shifted: first to her feet, then up at Billy, then back to her feet, then, imploringly, but silent, at Billy again. At times she managed a quick look toward the couch, more, I thought, toward Taylor than to me. Nothing but Eric's clock. We all heard that. There was nothing else for our ears.

Peggy coughed, then began to speak. Before she could, Billy burst: "Jesus. I really can't handle this. I don't know how to say this. I guess I should be flattered or something, but, shit, come on. I can't do it."

"Of course you can. Billy, just fuck me. Just fuck me. Please." Her voice faded a little after the first "fuck me."

"It is too weird. I can't handle it."

"I'm not trying anything funny, Billy. I have my diaphragm, it's still good. I'm not going to hound you or ruin your life. I just…I just need it. Please, Billy."

"I'm sorry. You're freaking me out. No. The answer is no." Almost faster than I could see, Billy, with guitar, was out of the room, his own bedroom door closing behind him. Not slammed, but distinctly shut.

Silence strutted back onstage. After a few minutes, Peggy began to cry, caught herself, sniffled, then cried again. Taylor and I continued our rigid pose until Taylor separated from me and slid to the floor in front of Peggy and took her hand. I followed, taking the other hand. Peggy's now-louder sobs subsided, and a bit more calmly she rubbed her sleeve across her eyes and cheeks. I remember noticing she had an embroidered blouse. That was unusual for her. She smiled, still teary:

"He must think I'm mad. Maybe I am."

We murmured negative noises.

"But I can't stand it. I'm hurting so much. I'm literally aching with loneliness. I paid twelve dollars for a massage in that place on Wilshire just to feel someone touch me. If I'm not mad, it is only a matter of time."

By now she was on the floor with us, alternately squeezing and dropping our hands. We were a tight circle, and again we became quiet, the emptiness punctuated occasionally by Peggy's heaving breaths. Another few minutes passed. She took one last calming breath, looked first at me, then at Taylor. She glanced down again and almost whispered:

"Taylor? What if…" but before I knew who she was addressing, much less what she was about to ask, Taylor ripped her hand from Peggy's and pulled herself and me to standing positions.

"No, Peggy. Don't even think about that. No. It's time for everyone to be where they belong, in their own beds."

With that, she opened the front door and added a rough "Good night" as Peggy, rising without another word, walked past her and across the Riveras' dark yard to her own room. Taylor closed the door, locked it, took my hand, and walked us deliberately to our room.

We fucked. Desperately. Without joy. Then Taylor slept, her back against me, but I remained awake, staring wide-eyed at nothing. Within a year, we would separate, painfully. In five years, we would each find our real, grown-up loves–both, it turned out, named Jenny–and become reasonably civil again. But in that moment with my right hand resting on Jenny's breast, I wondered at the depths of a person's hunger, and thought that if it had been me on the floor with a guitar, and Billy on the couch entwined with a girlfriend, *how would I have done?* For surely I would have done it, would have tried to fill that need in the night.

We never, ever talked about it. Eric never knew. We barely saw Peggy again. One time I saw her coming out of a bank. We both jumped, then with a half-laugh she said: "Don't worry, I'm not going to ask you for a favor," and scurried down the sidewalk. At Christmas, Taylor and I crossed the border for three drunken days in Ensenada, and Billy and Eric left town, too. We reassembled the day after New Year's, and as we paid the rent, Mr. Rivera told us that Peggy and her daughter had moved out. Once, three years ago, I'm sure I saw her at O'Hare in Chicago, but just as she was turning toward me I angled away and didn't look back.

Thank God I Saw Billy Sunday

Billy Sunday came to Burlington when I was fifteen. He was God in a gabardine suit. In Iowa. He demanded we save our souls. If we opened our hearts and walked with him, salvation was ours. I believe the first time I saw him I really did think it was Our Lord Himself in front of us, up on South Hill, just wearing modern clothes.

It was 1905, so that was fifty, no fifty-one years ago. I went with my grandmother every night. Now I'm older than she ever was. Everything was different for her. She was born in Pennsylvania in the middle of the Civil War. Her father never laid eyes on her, slaughtered at Gettysburg, all those bodies rotting on Independence Day. Her mother married again to a vicious man who dragged them all the way to the Mississippi, drinking and worse the whole way before she gave up and died, just thirty years old. She was only fourteen, my grandmother, when she paid a man to row her across the river almost exactly where the bridge is now, the very day her mother was buried. She told me she had no trouble living so close to Illinois as long as the Big Muddy was in between, and she never did see her stepfather again.

Imagine me at fifteen in my calico dress like those old photographs, every night in crowds the likes of which I had never experienced. Hear me now: Billy Sunday was your Elvis Presley on the Sullivan Show. He was Frankie Sinatra. He was Valentino and Rudy Vallee combined.

He hollered and strutted and preached for hours. "Christianity isn't for the weak or faint of heart—it isn't for hogs or weasels!" He'd been a famous baseball player, you know, before he found Christ. He said, and you could see it was true, that his body was his temple, a gift both from and for his maker. You saw his muscles bursting to break out of his suit and every night we got there early, front row. He was a handsome man. We didn't have microphones in those days but he didn't need one. I don't believe he even once used a megaphone.

Forty consecutive nights. I remember my grandmother sleeping almost the whole day, every day, thick brocade curtains drawn tight against her windows. She was already frail, her body ravaged by a life so much harder than mine, or yours. But at sundown she was the one leading us up the hill. By the end my grandmother had completely accepted her savior, which was a blessing because she lived only until the next spring, already had inside her whatever was killing her and probably knew it, too, though no one else did.

I am no longer inclined to rush to religion, but I remain grateful to Mr. Billy Sunday for what he gave my grandmother. She received every word and each found residence inside her heart. For me, it was my eyes, not my ears, that took him in, that conducted his energy into my body, and it was each animal step that pierced my body, that transformed me, over those summer nights, from an ignorant young girl to a sexual being. Billy Sunday never touched me, but every man who ever has should thank God I saw Billy Sunday. I know I do.

After the Whistle

A whistle had blown repeatedly—not the shift-change whistle but the alarm—and the town's people rushed toward it. Albert did not hear it. When his co-workers spoke of it later, after the funeral, they remarked how he had always "heard" whistles before, in some fashion none could explain. But not this time.

Waiting at the gate with the other wives, watching the insistent flames and then, as the fire fighters began to control things, the smoke that usurped the sky, Hazel had been fearful, but not overly so. Some women were frantic, wailing, sobbing. Her Albert was so cautious and even-tempered, unlike some of the other men who lived their lives as much in the bars as in their own homes, and often worked under the influence of—at best—terrible hangovers. He was not like that.

Quickly he was the sole missing worker, and then he was found. There were no cheers. Hazel felt what was found was not Albert at all, but a charred impostor of the man she loved. And yet she knew the truth. Two wives held her close as she squeezed shut her eyes and strove to remember something her father had said, either at the table or from the pulpit, that might be of use to her now. She could not.

The Viper's Smile

With the exception of the viper on the floor, it looked to be a lovely morning. The equinox moon, still present above the trees, had ushered a surprisingly early blue sky, empty of the week's overcast beginnings. Birdsong, now forty-seven days in, provided its familiar delicious welcome. But all of that was fiction now. Only the viper remained, curled in front of the door, perhaps a foot and a half long, if stretched for measuring, it was not fiction.

Mortality turns out to be a cold word after all. The cliché is true. While I'd slept, the viper had found a way into my hut to escape the night's chill. It is possible it had just entered, but more likely it owed a full night's rent. I shivered in the already warm Andalucia morning. What do I know about vipers? They are poisonous. Mortal. The only poisonous snake in Britain, I'd recently learned, but this was Spain, where it did not have the distinction of being the only one. But it didn't need to be the only one, as long as it *was* one, a deadly snake, and it most assuredly was. In my hut, curled, just inside the only door, mortality waited.

I sat on my cot, my arms locked around my knees, my back supported but not comforted by the wall. Comforting would have been a window behind me. What was the wall made of? Could I punch a hole in it, expand it, climb to liberation? For the first time I regretted not packing a sledge-hammer. Cumbersome, sure, and a tricky thing to get through security and customs, but right now it would trump every single dharma book I'd lugged from San Francisco to the Iberian Peninsula to this paradise near Alicante whose expiration date had suddenly imploded from October 1st to September 22nd. Just as with tofu or cottage cheese, you don't want to be around on the drop-dead date.

A true practitioner surely would have seized the opportunity, and meditated deeply. This was the stuff of legend, this was *my* time. But I just leaned against that wall.

The little desk where I did my writing and reading stood less than a foot from the viper. From my perch (I saw no percentage in stepping on the floor), when I was able to look away from my visitor I glanced at the surface of the desk, the words I'd intended to contemplate this morning in meditation: *The merit of a man who lives each day knowing it could be his last.*

Irony. Timing is everything, according to the comedians. I wasn't smiling but maybe the viper was. Can a viper smile? I didn't look. The viper remained. Smiling or not, it did nothing but remain. On a campus where I once taught, once a month every clock would freeze for two minutes, apparently to allow the system to correct itself. It is disconcerting to stare at a clock that will not advance. Students get nervous. Teachers, too. My clock said it had been eighteen minutes. The hut was a mile from its nearest neighbor in the secluded ravine, which up to this morning had been a stunningly peaceful home for me, ensconced among staggering granite walls just fifteen miles from the sea. There were no phones. I was on solitary retreat, my food delivered in a basket every ten days at the base of an almond tree. The delivery person was good: I had neither seen nor heard him. No one would look for me for another nine days, until the end of my time. If the viper did do its worst, though, it wouldn't matter a whole lot if anyone did come calling.

Eighteen minutes, in a certain light, is little different from a lifetime, and the room was bathed in that particular light.

And then I remembered the *New Yorker* cartoon. The one I'd taped to the outside of my laptop, which rested, its battery long dead, in its dusty carrying case just inches from the viper. The cartoon showed the classic Death figure, hooded and carrying his scythe, standing ominously at the side of a man sitting behind a desk, a computer in front of him, and the man looks up and says: "Thank God you've come. I can't get anything done without a deadline."

So I reached for my notebook and wrote these words. If anyone ever sees them, I thank you for your kind attention. May you be well.

Some Things

"Just tell me why a city in the middle of Ohio is called Columbus!" Jake's own history of countless History classes was on high alert. In another life he surely was a strutting rooster. Robby glanced at the rear-view mirror but Zelda was long gone. Jake's soundtrack spun on:

"Here's the deal. They name the city, not to mention a whole country in South America, for a guy who to his dying day thought he found India and named everybody Indians. And it wasn't just '1492 and sailed the ocean blue,' he crashed into this hemisphere four fucking times. He spotted Honduras once and said, 'Aha, I see China!' That was ten years *after* he saw Cuba and said the same thing. Cuba! You think Fidel Castro speaks Chinese?"

Robby guessed he probably didn't and the torrent continued. "If Columbus *had* discovered Ohio ten-to-one he'd have called it Korea. Why do we name things after him? My beautiful boots back there, I got 'em in Denton, Texas, right? Old Chris would say it was Mongolia. Shit, he might say my boots were pork chops. Never major in History, man, it can depress you.

Jake slumped in his shotgun seat and the bus rolled onward, the odometer taking them east one click at a time.

Two hours and 85 miles later, bedding down in a rest stop packed with yet another collection of heavy-breathing truck-trailers, Robby was picturing Zelda listening to the tape and thinking about him when Jake muttered "Damn. That chick stole my boots."

The next morning was only a short drive, heading for a promised crash pad. They could use showers. Robby doubted Jake remembered showers. The Madison house had been the best of the trip except it contained so many real occupants that they never had a chance at the hot water. Maybe his road buddy had showered in Missouri.

"God, I'd love to stand right where they got shot!" Robby cringed at the memory of the hitchhiker's words, the one who had gotten off when they left I-70. The guy had almost pissed in his pants when

151

Robby said they were heading to Kent. He absolutely did intend to see where they got shot but he didn't think it would be all that cool. He drove north on 43 looking for Main Street and the right turn toward University Avenue, and then the address itself scribbled on a recent *Rolling Stone* with Janis on the cover. He figured this might be the fifth University Avenue of the trip. Notorious Kent, with 28,000 normal residents, plus its twenty-odd thousand students. Kent State University.

And one more thing he'd tried to recall yesterday, but couldn't, during Jake's Columbus parade. Too late, of course, he remembered. From *I Love Lucy:* "Look, all I know is that Columbus discovered Ohio in 1776." It might have been Desi, might have been Lucy. Either way, he'd find a way to use it.

For once the directions made sense and they found the house on the first try. They were admitted by a bleary-eyed guy called Charlie who was not the connection on this side, and who hadn't heard of their coming, but he vaguely ushered them into a room where he thought they'd be sleeping and left them there. It was in the back, behind the kitchen, and empty except for a sagging couch that exploded with dust as soon as their backpacks landed on it, and a blue milk crate holding a television with rabbit ears. Jake claimed first dibs on the shower, to be followed by "nothing, I'm just going to crash for a little." Robby hid his shock and immediately walked out to explore the town, and with even more curiosity than usual, the campus itself.

Four dead, right here.

It was just a town, a little town, nothing more. He was no expert on Ohio but this is probably what it was supposed to look like. This had been the firestorm that inflamed every campus from coast to coast? May 4th wasn't even six months back. UCLA had shut down for weeks, wiping out spring quarter, classes and finals fading into haphazard essays mailed to professors in exchange for postcards with pass-fail grades. But this was just a town.

Musing on perception, projection and reality, words he'd picked up in Philosophy 70 and lovingly caressed whenever he remembered them, he abruptly found himself at a campus entrance called Prentice Gate. His instincts had served him well. All he had done was float until he encountered a line of students, a process more to his liking than checking his progress by street signs or city maps. Whatever his navigation faults on the open road, and he had plenty, here he was captain of his ship. Ahead of him six or eight students were at a standstill. The first in line was producing identification and the others already had wallets or cards out for display. It looked like a ticket gate but this was no rock show. Behind him, two students wore their KSU identities around their necks. How did you get a guest pass, if that's what he needed? He should have asked the guy at the house, but never would he have imagined needing one. Wasn't this a public school? He hesitated as the couple behind him passed him, passed inspection, and then walked toward a library. Now there was only the monitor, a woman his mother's age in a skirt and grey blouse, a nametag reading "Beshirs," and, below the name, "Campus Security."

"No," she said, "guest passes do not exist. Only those individuals with current university identification are allowed on the grounds. There are no exceptions. Were your sister a valid student, or even a staff member, you could not accompany her."

"What if," he smiled in what he hoped was an engaging manner, "what if I were a visiting scholar, here to consult with a colleague in the Chemistry Department, for example? What then?"

"As you don't appear to be one, it's an academic question, isn't it?" Mrs. Beshirs gave a small smile in response. "In fact, if you were my own son, I couldn't let you in. If I did," her voice lowered, "each of us would be forced to contend with one of them." She nodded behind her. Just out of view unless you looked carefully, two soldiers casually stood, as casually as any people with real rifles can stand. He gasped. He tried to think when he'd last seen a rifle in real life. He wasn't sure that he had.

"Unbelievable," he muttered.

"And they, as well as *my* colleagues, are at every gate. I'm sorry young man, but unless you choose to enroll, you may proceed no further."

Other students, real students, were approaching. He wandered away from the gate, found a bench and sat with his head in his hands. Armed guards. Soldiers! The infamous Ohio National Guard, he supposed. He shivered. He didn't know what he'd been expecting but he knew to a cold certainty what he hadn't. Were they the same ones who'd shot and killed? It's a *state college*, right? It isn't exactly Saigon. Why are they still here? Are they proud, just sticking around because they won? Damn Governor Rhodes. Damn Richard Nixon. Damn all of them. The hitchhiker would be disappointed, and now he really did want to walk where they walked, stand where they fell. Why was he in Kent if not for that?

If it could happen here, not just could, it did happen here, it obviously could happen anywhere in Nixon's new *Amerika*. He rose from the bench, carrying his jacket this time, sweating in his clammy t-shirt despite the cool October air.

He walked in circles, squares, shapes without direction, burning frustration until his inner magnet located a burger joint. It was almost two, most tables empty after any lunch-rush that might have been, and he stepped in for his first meal of the day. The stroll had helped. A burger and fries, comfort food in any state, waited just inside, and he entered *Orville's*.

While he ate he pulled out the postcard he'd picked up near Columbus yesterday, in the truck stop where they'd dropped the envious hitcher. It was the perfect choice for his mom. This was his first time in Ohio but his mom was a native and a sometimes-proud alumna of Ohio State University. Only sometimes, because on football Saturdays she rooted fiercely against her *alma mater*, so strong was her animosity for Coach Woody Hayes. "An embarrassment. Nothing but an embarrassment." She disapproved of merging college football, which she enjoyed, with martial law, which she felt should be reserved for things more serious than blocking and tackling. She checked the schedules each week and loudly rooted for whoever was playing the Buckeyes. And whoever played Notre Dame, too. Nobody rooted for Notre Dame. You might as well be a Yankee fan for all the sport in that.

The card was a color photo of the Ohio State marching band forming a cursive "*Ohio*" on the fifty-yard line, just as the tuba player, it was always the tuba player, was racing to dot the "i." Family legend had it that her father, also a Columbus native, had also attended Ohio State, but only for one month. After an afternoon spent marching with the Ohio State band in the cavernous Michigan stadium, while on the train back from Ann Arbor and in the midst of post-game revelry, he had completely misplaced his bass drum. As a result, he'd been invited to leave the band. In response, he left the university. So went the story.

He kept his message postcard-light but did acknowledge, as the postmark would confirm, being in Kent, but just noted that "everything is quiet and the campus is closed to outsiders." He mentioned chugging through Columbus "in the slow lane," and scribbled that he'd sent "evil thought-daggers to Woody." He closed with "Jesse sends his love." Jesse Owens, the Gold Medalist in Hitler's Olympics of '36, had attended both East High and Ohio State when she did, though they moved in different circles once they hit college. If she'd married the black sprinter, he argued, not only would he boast a much better tan, he also wouldn't have been the slowest runner on his high school baseball team.

He looked across to a Kent State football schedule taped on the wall next to the Coke machine. Why was he thinking about high school baseball in Kent, Ohio? Wasn't he too young for nostalgia? Postcard in hand he walked to the bulletin board. He flashed on a poster for a Jefferson Airplane concert here but it had already happened. That would have been something, to see the Airplane in Kent. Then he found a flyer with a review by some New York critic for the movie *Soldier Blue*, and the italicized words: *Stained with the Blood of the Innocent.* He thought of Jake's ministerial pronouncement back in L.A. that *he* would *never* see it. His pal was more than just a Dean's List scholar in

History, he was a movie snob: "If it's made in America, somebody's got to *pay me* to see it." The movie was playing around the corner but he wasn't buying. He was fine with American movies but violence scared him wherever it was, on screen or not.

What world was this that beckoned him to adulthood? Indians slaughtered. Jews gassed. Bombs and napalm and Kent State. And Jackson State, too, don't forget. Which he had, again. Where was Jackson State? Black students getting shot wasn't cool enough to stay in the news, he guessed, but he had some responsibility to remember on his own. Wasn't the twentieth century supposed to be about progress? It was screwed. He grabbed a bottle of Black Label from the cooler, dropped cash on the counter, and sat back at "his" table. His beard made him look old enough to buy booze, a comfort to any bartender or server who cared about such things. He still had a few fries waiting for him.

He nursed the beer. Mostly he held the chilled bottle to his forehead. Violent movies were nothing new, what could be new about cowboys and Indians, or more accurately, Cavalry and Indians? Violence in real life, his life, hadn't intruded much. He'd seen cops clubbing kids during a street protest, and watched one drunken brawl in the parking lot of a high school football game with flying rocks and ice-chests and fists pounding into faces. And, once, his first week of college, a vicious girl-fight in his dormitory elevator. He'd been pinned to the wall, more stunned than scared, but one of them had blood pouring out of her eye. She quit school immediately and the other was kicked out, arrested probably.

He walked again to the postings on the wall. This time he found something that referred to May 4th, a theatre production called *A Garden in Kent*. The graphic was a row of rifles shown from the side, standing upright in a field. On top of each bayonet was a flower. Whatever it was, it had run a month ago, even earlier than the Airplane show. Ohio bulletin boards were as up-to-date as California's.

His fingers traced each flower. Roses, he was pretty sure. It was in black and white so they weren't the red of the Grateful Dead, but they were certainly roses. He clenched his fists, opened them, clenched again. He sighed, looked once more at the poster, touched it again, and turned back to his table.

"I can take you there."

Robby looked toward the voice. In the shadows of a corner booth, its table covered with papers, folders, and index cards, sat a thin man, the man who must have spoken.

"What did you say?"

"I said 'I can get you in. I can take you there.' You want to go, don't you?"

"Yeah. Shit, yeah. I want to go. But I can't..."

Interrupting, the man droned a fair imitation of Mrs. Beshirs: "You cannot go because you're not a student. You are not 'affiliated' with the university. Any person found on campus without express permission of the Regents—that is, without proper and current identification—shall be arrested for trespass and prosecuted to the fullest extent of the law."

"How'd you know I wasn't a student?"

"Students don't write postcards."

"Do you have some I.D.'s, some fake identification? Is that how? Can you get me in that way?"

"Not a chance. They're on those like white on rice. They'll bust you for forgery, too, and that's a felony. But I know a way."

He studied the man. He was older, maybe even 30, with an impressive Fu Manchu moustache, the tails dripping below his chin. His sideburns were thick and his brown hair was tied in a ponytail that fell a few inches below his collar. He wore a grey work shirt and over that, an army surplus bomber jacket, almost identical to his own. His, purchased in an Army-Navy store back home, cost three bucks and he wore it whenever the temperature was below 72. It was on the back of his chair right now, over at his table.

"Grab a seat," the guy said. "Wait, get me a brew, would you? I'm a little short today."

"No problem, I'll be right back." He bought two more beers, grabbed his jacket on the way back and slid in across from his new acquaintance.

"I'm Robby, man. From California." He reached across for a full soul-shake.

"They just call me Guevara."

They clanged bottles, drank.

"You gonna get drafted? Kid, if you don't got a 2-S, you're gonna be up shit creek in one hell of a hurry."

"Damn straight about that. But I got one. I'm just stopping out for a quarter. Road-tripping. I go back in January. UCLA."

"'Stopping out.' That's good. I guess that's what I'm doing, too, but I'm not going back in January or fucking ever. UCLA, huh. More like the U. of Saigon for me. If I went back, which I ain't."

Could that jacket have been *issued* to him, not bought in a strip mall? The nametag was missing, had been torn off, which didn't mean anything. His was no different.

"Were you in the Army?"

Guevara laughed without smiling: "Did the Pope crap in the woods? Right on I was in it: nine months, six days, and one medal until I skipped my free flight back to sunny Southeast Asia. Uncle Sam had me long enough."

"Did you get some kind of discharge?"

"Not likely. They'll lock my ass up if they find me. I'm not letting that happen. I learned a few things over there in the way of observation, survival skills. I'll give the Army credit, they taught me some good shit."

"Are you from around here?"

"Nope."

"What are you doing now?" He bit his tongue. What was he now, a cub reporter? He couldn't suppress the thrill of meeting a real deserter. It was too bad Jake wasn't here but he was sure glad that *he* was.

"Stuff. I'm working with some people. Like I said, I learned some things. Look at this."

He pulled out a typed piece of paper.

"It's a copy of what I sent to General Westmoreland himself, and to Nixon. Those ones had my real name. I covered it up when I made these copies."

Robby began to read:

A Soldier's Declaration

I am making this statement as an act of wilful defiance of military authority, because I believe the war is being deliberately prolonged by those who have the power to end it.

On behalf of those who are suffering now I make this protest against the deception which is being practised on them; also I believe that I may help to destroy the callous complacence with which the majority of those at home regard the continuance of agonies which they do not share, and which they have not sufficient imagination to realize.

As always, he read too quickly, so when he hit the "not sufficient imagination to realize," he started over, this time slowly, savoring it word by word. He felt blessed to read it, twice-blessed to be in the presence of its creator.

"Far-out! You should send one to every paper in the country. Is that why you have all these copies?"

"Nah, only Nixon and Westmoreland got 'em in their mailboxes. Besides, papers want your real name. I give them away but I ask for a little green to help me do what I'm doing. You don't get a paycheck in my line of work."

He had to mean the *Underground*. A mythic word. Robby searched his pocket for some dollar bills but found only coins. He pried his wallet from his back pocket, made a quick calculation, and pulled out a five.

"Here. Will this do? But could I have two?"

"That's fine. I appreciate it." He watched as *Guevara* was scrawled across the bottom of the page.

"Thanks man." Un-fucking believable. He'd have a tale to tell the history scholar, the master of the nap.

"You sure you want to go to campus?" As the man spoke he looked directly at him. "It's heavy. I've seen people freak out."

"I'm cool. I want to go. I can't be this close and not go."

Guevara gathered his papers and folders, stuffed them in his backpack, and snapped up his jacket. "I'll just piss away this beer first," he said, and walked toward the back.

Robby drummed his fingers on the table, now empty except for two bottles, the battle-weary ashtray, and the coffee mug surrounded by the residue of three packs of sugar. For a moment he wondered if the man might have slipped out a back door and that the offer to take him to campus, to the scene of the crime, was a bunch of crap, but the wait wasn't too long and together they walked outside and down a couple of familiar blocks south before entering uncharted territory. They walked without speaking for twenty minutes before his guide stopped for a full minute before whispering: "Follow me." They sidled between a fence and a hedge and scurried over crackling dry leaves in the shadow of a white house. He worried about the noise but worried more about mentioning the noise. They were on another property now, then another. The guy knew what he was doing, didn't pause once, and before he even realized it, they were actually on campus, dormitories off to their right.

"So much for security," Guevara puffed. They were probably safe now, as they looked like anybody else. Unless somebody demanded identification. That would be a problem.

"I was there, you know." The voice was low and Robby, breathing a little hard from the last rush through underbrush, almost missed it

"You mean, when it went down?"

"I'd seen crazy shit in 'Nam, lots of it, but this fucking blew my mind."

160

On open ground now, hopefully beyond all checkpoints, they walked among students. Robby bought two cokes at a coke shack and they rested on a bench, Guevara's eyes far away. Anxious as he was to get to the spot, he yearned for more testimony and told himself to be patient.

At last Guevara spoke and here he was without a tape recorder.

"I pulled into town in April. Stuff was happening and I wanted to check it out. Anyway, my truck wasn't going any further. It's good to sit. I got some metal in me and motion aggravates it." They'd crawled through a hole in one fence before scaling a higher one. He was again grateful to the man.

"You know that the ROTC building was torched a couple of nights before, right after Nixon sent troops into fucking Cambodia. That's what set things off, Cambodia. What are they thinking? 'Hey, Spiro, the war's not going so good, let's invade somebody else?' You can't make this stuff up!"

He gestured toward an expanse of green, and continued: "Even with Cambodia on all the news, though, it was a strange scene here. Riots down on Water Street, but up here there was a carnival. I mean a real one with kids and dogs and balloons and shit. And the ROTC building had been torched a day or two before–it was still smoking! Just nuts. Then came the Monday, May 4th. They talk about Pearl Harbor being a 'Day of Infamy.' We had our own, right here. Thank you Richard Nixon, you did what we couldn't do, you brought the war home."

"It was around noon, right?"

"Yeah, about then, but nobody was looking at watches. It was just the usual crap: the Guard marching, the kids running and shouting like they were playing cops and robbers, and then some bonehead started shooting. And since they were trained about as well as pound puppies, a bunch more joined in. I hit the dirt by that bush over there, not that it would have done me any good. I did figure that most of them were firing high, but all it takes is one. It stopped, and a body was down in front of me. I didn't know his name then but I knew he was one dead freak. I had a medic buddy so I know some stuff, but not enough to bring that boy back. A bunch of bodies were down and chicks were screaming. It could have gotten worse but people calmed down. To fight another day."

"What did you do?"

"I started thinking about we needed to do to get to that day. I got off campus because I didn't need to be showing my I.D. any more than was necessary. It was new and I wanted to keep it clean. That night, all everyone thought was 'Nixon's blown it now.' The town called a curfew but everyone said 'fuck it,' and kept walking and talking until dawn. I personally stayed in the background but the whole place was ripe for burning."

"Yeah, we went pretty wild in L.A., right after. We were on a righteous rampage, maybe going to hit the bank, but it didn't last long. Almost got arrested that day. Probably should have." He recalled the cat and mouse games with the cops, the thrill he'd felt as he taunted and ran.

"But it's going to be a long haul," Guevara went on. "It's like Mao or the Viet Cong, if you want a real revolution you got to take one mother of a long view. And you're going to lose people along the way. It'll take," and again, he looked straight at him, "a shitload of martyrs. People have to understand that what happened here was a good thing, a real good thing."

Except for a furtive grab of a few blades of grass, which he quickly let float away with the breeze, and which he just as quickly regretted not stuffing into his pocket, Robby hadn't moved. Guevara stood, rubbed the back of his right leg, and said "time to go." They walked out the same gate where earlier he'd been denied entry. Security wasn't paid to keep people in, and it was a different guard this time anyway. When they reached Orville's, Guevara stopped outside the door, his right hand tight on Robby's elbow.

"Listen, man, I hate to ask, but can you front me something more? I'm running two guys to Canada next week and my starter's still messed up. I can fix it myself but the parts are a bitch. You don't want

162

to break down with that kind of cargo. I understand if you can't, but if you can help…?"

Even before the word "help" Robby was pulling another five from his wallet.

"Right on." Guevara faded into the evening dusk. Robby exhaled deeply three times and stepped inside once again.

He went straight to the corner table, "Guevara's Table." He started to wonder about the guy's real name but quickly dismissed as juvenile the need to know, and pulled out and re-read the stunning "Soldier's Declaration." Guevara was a Soldier and a Man and he saw that maybe he could develop into such a man. He imagined not going back to school in January. Maybe it was time to leave the nest. There was work to be done. High-pitched laughter interrupted his thoughts and he looked up to see his closest friend walking in with another guy, a pale guy who turned out to be Nathan, who was the connection between here and Madison.

Jake laughed even more when he spotted him, and immediately bought three beers. He actually was old enough. "This is just the beginning," he said as he reached the table. "I think we're going to drink tonight." He lifted one of the bottles, swept it broadly as if toasting the street outside, and announced: "No miserable-way are we in Kansas anymore. This is one heavy scene."

"That's no lie. Look at this." He pushed Guevara's *Declaration* toward him and then pumped right hands with Nathan.

Jake glanced at it. "Yeah, this is cool. You know what it is, don't you?"

"Well, shit, yeah," he said. "The guy who wrote it just gave it to me. He was sitting right here, he's underground, calls himself Guevara, but of course that's not his real name. He got me onto campus and he's running guys to Canada!" He paused for breath, for questions, for exclamations. But his listeners did not play. They said nothing. Then Jake spoke:

"Man, I know you don't go to class much, but you do know Siegfried Sassoon, don't you? World War One poet?"

"German, right? I remember Wilfred Owen, but he was English and got killed practically on Armistice Day. Or was that the guy in *All Quiet on the Western Front*?"

"No, Toto, Sassoon was a Brit, too, despite the Siegfried thing, and he wrote this. Try 1917, give or take. He was an officer in the trenches and he got tossed in the loony bin 'cuz he wouldn't shut up. But *he* wrote it." Jake waited a couple of beats. "Do your goddamn reading. Isn't that why you're an English major, because you like to read?"

"No way. You're wrong this time. He did. He told me. And anyway, he was here, I mean there, on the grass, when they were shooting. He almost got shot. He took me there. He was sitting where you are, this is his table."

"Rob, some things are worth learning, and…"

Nathan picked up the thread. He spoke with the same New York accent as two of the guys in Madison.

"Whoever 'Guevara' is, whatever his name is," he said, "he wasn't on campus. He showed up later. A lot of guys did, that next week, but most of them have moved on. Show's over, right? Maybe he was in the army, maybe not, who's going to ask for proof? I don't know why he's still here. No, that's wrong, he's got good reason. You know that 'girls say yes to boys who say no' thing? I've seen him walk out of here with some fine-looking chicks."

He cradled his beer. Time stumbled. He heard more New York rhythms.

"There's another guy who claims that he was *with* the Guard that day, but he didn't fire, and that he's AWOL now. I don't know how much action he's getting but it's got to be more than me."

"But…" But he didn't know what to ask. Had Guevara been in 'Nam? Had he just been ripped off for ten bucks? Had he even seen *the place*?

"Just sip it slow, *mi amigo*." Jake patted his shoulder. "Ain't nothin' but a history lesson, no tuition required."

It wasn't a sippy cup but it might as well have been. He sipped.

At the Station

He sat directly across from me though the Córdoba station waiting area was packed with a dozen rows of unoccupied benches. I had sixteen minutes before it was my turn to pass through the sliding-glass doors and onto the platform, doors guarded by serious men with rifles, doors that separated those who waited from those who actually went somewhere.

Next to me, my duffel. Next to him, nothing. Traveling light, or he was meeting someone. Either was possible, not everyone was as restless as me.

The message board flashed arrivals, mostly from Seville. One in four minutes, another in sixteen, and a third in half an hour. And from Madrid, eight minutes.

Over the top of *mi periódico* I caught the man's eyes, or rather I stared head-on into his eyes, but though his eyes were equally locked on mine, they shared nothing, no sign of connection. Was he blind? *Ciega*, a word I had just learned: *ciega*–blind. I glanced away but curiosity conquered shame and I looked again, this time less directly.

His skin told tales I couldn't read. I guessed he had been a child in the Civil War, perhaps a child-soldier.

The doors opened just enough and a throng poured through, the gap so narrow that each person had to walk single-file. He turned his body and I watched as he scrutinized each Seville arriving passenger. Not blind, then, and not going anywhere.

Then I saw it. He pulled a black-and-white photo from a jacket pocket. Three-by-five, or its Spanish equivalent, and he held it almost at arm's length. My opinion of his vision clouded again. Because he shifted position, I easily saw the photo, perhaps better than he could. The two figures in it could be, but weren't, Frank Sinatra and Dean Martin, fifty years back, so swaggering their stance, their fearless grins bursting with life. Virility. One's hand was on the other's shoulder and the posture boasted of primacy and the unquestioned glory of youth.

He studied it. Put it back in his pocket. Lit a cigarette but immediately pinched it cold. In three minutes the photo was out again, studied again. Another train, and another burst of people. He stared at each, but found no one.

Is today the day? He got up, walked just outside the door, and re-lit his cigarette. The next Seville train was fifteen minutes away. He puffed rapidly and was back in two minutes, a faithful dog at his window. He consulted the photo.

My train was announced, arrived, and left for Madrid without me. There will be another. The afternoon would be spent watching the man watch the arrivals and checking the photo, and remembering, both of us, those moments that would live now only in our memories, our pockets, and in our bordered photographs. It stares back at us, challenges us, demands we seek vision we once held.

Acknowledgements

Heartfelt thanks to my writing mentors, especially the majestic teacher Amber Dermont, who has taught me so much. I have been inspired by the writer/humanitarian Luis Alberto Urrea, and by the generosity and encouragement of Robin Stratton. Further credit goes to the poet/novelist–Stephen Parr (Ananda) and to the late poet David Keefe (Manjusvara). Also, Jeanne Althouse, Kalpana Mohan, Pam Parker, and Aggie Zivaljevic, each of whom has made me a better reader, and thus, a better writer. And, as always, Karunadevi.

.

About the Author

Tony Acarasiddhi Press lives near San Francisco and tries to pay attention. Sometimes he does.

During a period of meditation on a retreat in 2003 he could barely sit still because a story was spilling into his consciousness. At the final bell he raced outside and wrote it down as fast as he could. He's been writing ever since, primarily short stories, but also poems and essays. Since 2004 his efforts have appeared online and in print close to 100 times, including journals from at least five different countries. In 2014, *Boston Literary Magazine* nominated one of his stories for the Pushcart Prize. A few years earlier, *JMWW* had nominated another story for the Million Writers Award.

He continues to follow a Buddhist path (hence the name *Acarasiddhi*), and struggles to sit still even without the intrusion of a story. His personal mantra is "keep walking" and he will do that as long as he can.

www.ingramcontent.com/pod-product-compliance
Lightning Source LLC
Chambersburg PA
CBHW050749250626
47155CB00005B/1983